*StarLords*

# Shy Talent

BIANCA D'ARC

This book is a work of fiction. The names, characters, places, and incidents are products of the writer's imagination or have been used fictitiously and are not to be construed as real. Any resemblance to persons, living or dead, actual events, locale or organizations is entirely coincidental.

No part of this book may be used or reproduced in any manner whatsoever without written permission, except in the case of brief quotations embodied in critical articles and reviews.

# DEDICATION

With my deepest thanks to Jess Bimberg, my once and future editor, Peggy McChesney, who is a marvelous sounding board and cheerleader, and Valerie Tibbs for making such lovely covers for these books. You guys are awesome.

And as always, special thanks to my family – especially my dad who instilled a love of science and science fiction in me from an early age. Most kids can't say their dads are rocket scientists. I'm one of the lucky ones who can say that for a fact. You rock, Dad!

.

# CHAPTER ONE

"Bettsua! I'm talking to you. Now pay attention."

The scolding voice was one Bet was well familiar with. Even though she was officially a Specitar now, her aunt still had a way of making her feel about two years old.

"Yes, Aunt Petra. I heard you. I'll be sure to take my warm sweater with me on my new assignment."

It was the ugliest sweater in creation, but her aunt had bought it for her, so Bet had to wear it, and let the old woman see her in it. Too bad other people had to see her in it too. The drab color and baggy fit only made her more of an oddball than she already was. Even among Specitars, she was considered strange, and that was saying something.

Immense telekinetic power and not much else to call her own, that's what she had. At least, nothing she could claim publicly. If others knew what else she could do, her life would probably be even more difficult than it already was.

Bet sighed, packing the ugly sweater, along with others like it, in the small valise she would take on board with her when she left on her first offworld mission. He aunt didn't allow the more stylish clothing that might show off some of Bet's curves—if she'd had any curves, that is. Bet was too tall. She didn't have hips to speak of, though she felt a little overdeveloped in the chest area. Shy about the huge breasts and above average height that had always made her feel like a freak, she habitually slouched, hiding behind baggy, concealing clothes and thick glasses she didn't really need.

Oh, as a child she'd been too young for the simple corrective surgery on her eyes, but she'd had the procedure done a few years ago with complete success. She wore lenses now only out of habit and a desire to maintain the status quo.

People had gotten used to seeing her in her old-fashioned glasses and baggy clothes. To take them off now might give people the impression she was trying to look sexy or something, and she couldn't bear to hear the inner commentary such a thought might inspire in the catty women she worked with.

For that was the other major Talent Bet had, though she dearly wished at times it had never developed. She could hear other people's thoughts. Or, at least, she could hear those of non-Talented and lesser-Talented people relatively easily. Those with stronger Talents than her own were harder to hear because higher-level Talents usually had stronger shielding, making it a pleasure for her to be around them.

Which was why she'd jumped at the chance to work for the Council. Mages were always well shielded, and even though just lately she'd been picking up on more and more of their thoughts too, the job she'd been doing for them, while not too exciting, had kept her away from lesser-Talents as much as possible.

But her Talent had recently jumped up another notch, and she feared soon even the haven of the Mage's Council would be denied her as those Mages' shields became inadequate to protect her from hearing their thoughts. The offworld trip aboard the newly christened research vessel *Calypso* had been offered to her at just the right time, and she'd been thrilled by the idea that she might be able to get away for a while and sort out her enhanced abilities.

Plus, she'd get to work with Lord Agnor. Her heart did a little flip when she thought of the tall, quiet man with the kind eyes. He was the most powerful Specitar of the current generation, and new head of the Specitar's enclave. But he'd also recently been made a StarLord and given command of the *Calypso*. He had a great deal of offworld experience, and with all that had been happening—the attacks on Council worlds and the renewed threat from the Wizards' collective and their allies—the Mage Council had asked him to assemble a crew and take to the stars.

She had no idea how or why she'd been chosen to take part in the mission, but she wasn't about to ask. She wanted off this planet and away from the people she could all too easily read. No one knew yet about this jump in her power. She'd been careful to hide it, lest they make her undergo more testing.

She feared that, if the Council knew she could sometimes hear some of their thoughts, they'd terminate her employment, and she had no idea what she'd do then. She needed the job. She was the only breadwinner in her family, and she had to support her aunt and the small dwelling they rented.

Going offworld for a bit sounded like the perfect solution. The advance on salary alone would pay their rent for a year. And being near Lord Agnor didn't hurt either.

The man probably didn't even know she existed, but she'd watched him from afar for many months. Since he'd come back from that mission with the newly made Shas, Lord Micah and his wife, Jeri, Bet had watched their friend Agnor. He had come back from that voyage changed in a way that made even the other Specitars look at him with new respect.

It was said he had used his incredibly strong telepathic Talent to communicate all the way from Liata, an agricultural planet on the fringes of Council space. She'd heard the stories about how the ship he'd been on then, the *Circe*, had been hit by a powerful psi wave and all aboard had been changed. The captain and his mate, Lord Micah and Lady Jeri, had been gifted with Sha level power—the highest of all the Talent rankings—and all the rest of the crew had jumped up in rank from what they'd been.

The current captain of the *Circe*, Lord Darak, had risen from a high-level Dominar to Master Mage in a heartbeat, skipping right over the rank of Mage to Master Mage. The younger crewmen had also jumped one or two ranks overnight. But what had happened to Lord Agnor was something the enclave was still trying to figure out.

It appeared no one knew how to classify Lord Agnor's immense leap in power. Specitars didn't really have a lot of further delineation of their ranks. They were all just really, really good at one particular thing, and that made them a Specitar. Lord Agnor's primary Talent was telepathy. Bet's was telekinesis. She could lift huge loads with just a thought, and that was pretty nifty, even she had to admit, but the other thing—the hearing people's thoughts thing—that had been more a curse than a gift.

With this new ability, she could hear what they really thought about her. Oh, some people were kind, but most were pitying, and many were just plain mean. Her aunt didn't love her at all, she knew. The old woman viewed Bet as a responsibility she'd had to take on when her brother and sister-in-law had died. She also saw Bet as a sort of safety net for when she grew too old to take care of herself, but there was no real love there. Her aunt hadn't cared for her brother's wife, and Bet apparently looked just like her.

The men she worked with were kind but often thought of her clothing with unkind amusement and, in a few cases, pity. She heard their unkind thoughts as she struggled to hide her feelings. And the women she worked with—two, in particular—were just downright mean. Alis and Nanci made cutting remarks to her face about her clothes while, in their minds, they ripped her to shreds at just about every encounter. They were jealous of her power, which was stronger and more useful than theirs. In a way, the jealousy was flattering, but they were really catty about it, and their thoughts and remarks about her appearance hurt her terribly.

Not that she'd ever let them realize it. Those two probably wouldn't care if they learned she could hear their thoughts, but Bet hoped other people would be ashamed at knowing that she heard every unkind thought they had about her. Even her supervisor, old Dominar Reginalt, had thought some unkind things about the way she looked and had even questioned why she would be selected for such a plum offworld assignment when he'd come to tell her about it. Outwardly happy for her, inside, he was thinking that she'd mess up somehow and that there were other candidates better suited for the position.

She didn't let her disappointment in his true thoughts show on her face. She knew he was making an effort to be kind outwardly, and that he'd feel really bad if he knew she knew what he was really thinking. That's why this so-called gift was more of a curse. She didn't want to know people's innermost thoughts. She just wanted to be left alone.

* * *

Agnor looked over the crew lists as he took his command chair for the very first time. The *Calypso* was a brand new ship, ostensibly a science and exploration vessel, but with a dual purpose. He'd spent too many years aboard the *Circe*, a merchanter that did double duty as a spy ship, not to look forward to his own foray into the dark world of secret plots and plans.

Few people realized he'd specifically chosen every member of the crew himself. When you were going to be cooped up in a relatively small ship with the same people for months on end, you wanted to make sure they were people you could get along with. Sharing pleasure among the crew was a given, so he'd tried to pick a good complement of males and females who were reasonably compatible. That meant finding people of similar Talent rankings—or as close as he could manage. He'd probably have to oversee a few first joinings to make sure nobody got hurt, but he didn't mind that in the least.

In fact, he was looking forward to it. Especially when his eyes settled on one particular name on his crew list.

Bettsua Malkin.

He'd seen her in action, though she probably didn't realize it. A few months ago, there'd been a terrible accident on the roadway just outside the Council compound. Agnor had just sent for help telepathically when he felt a huge surge of psi power from the other side of the wide road. And there stood little Bettsua, guiding the huge freight hauler off the smaller vehicle, tossing them around in the air as if they were toys and placing them gently on the roadway, safely apart and right side up. She hadn't even broken a sweat, and then, she'd left quickly, not sticking around to see what would happen next.

He'd thought that odd enough that he took the time to look into her personnel file. She hadn't been tested in quite some time, and he found that odd, as well. The last testing she'd had didn't indicate nearly enough power to do what she'd done with those heavy vehicles. He sensed she was hiding her obvious increase in power for some reason. He also sensed an aloneness in her he recognized well from his own existence. Before he'd joined the crew of the *Circe* and found acceptance there, he'd felt very alone—as she must feel, so young, so powerful, and so isolated.

Agnor had learned more about her home life, and his heart had gone out to the tall, shy young woman who had lost her mother and father so early in life. He didn't know why he was so drawn to her, but it was an inexplicable feeling he didn't question. He'd requested her for his crew without any further consideration. In fact, hers was the first name on the list when he'd been asked to draw one up. Eyebrows had been raised by his choice, but he stood firm. He wanted her on his crew. He wanted a chance to get to know her, perhaps share pleasure with her, and learn what hid beneath her protective outer shell.

Agnor hadn't been the first aboard, but much of the crew was still arriving as the ship prepared for its maiden voyage. This ship was quite different from the *Circe*, but the bridge crew stations were similar. There was a nav station to Agnor's far right where Dominar Petris Galeger would plot their course. There was also a pilot's chair at the nose of the triangular bridge from which Authoritar Jemin Fortuna would guide the ship, and a comm station to Agnor's left that would be manned by his former student, Specitar Brennin Dale. The weapons station to Agnor's immediate right would be home to his Executive Officer, Specitar Lilith Cole.

She was one of the few people Agnor counted among his friends. She specialized in seeing probable outcomes and had a penchant for science and math, though her Talent seemed more metaphysical than scientific. Foretelling the future had always been a rare gift, and it was Lilith's strongest Talent, though unlike most Specitars, she had a secondary ability of reasonably strong telepathy. She was older than most of the crew, older than Agnor himself, but she was a steady, likeable woman who was tough in a crisis and had a very useful Talent.

Making her his Executive Officer had also raised eyebrows, but this was his ship, and he wouldn't be told how to run it. Lilith had a big heart and a kind soul, and she would help this odd group solidify into something more like the family atmosphere he'd experienced aboard the *Circe*. At least he hoped it would work out that way.

Agnor himself was a quiet man, and he knew he could never fill the almost fatherly role his old friend, Micah, had taken on as captain of the *Circe*. Micah had forged the crew of that ship into a family, and Agnor felt he didn't have the ability to do the same without a little help. He also didn't have the sheer charisma of the *Circe's* current captain, his friend, the rogue Mage Master Darak. Agnor had always lived in the shadows of Micah and Darak. He knew he would need Lilith's special charm if the crew of the *Calypso* was to be forged into a family.

Lilith would be the mom, the caretaker of the group. She wasn't old, by any means, rather it was her kind heart that made people want to befriend her. In fact, she was gorgeous, though kind of short. At least a foot and a half shorter than himself, Lilith's big personality made people think she was taller, or so she cheerfully insisted. She had beautiful curly red hair and sparkling bright green eyes, as well as a voluptuous body she knew how to dress. She wasn't overly suggestive with her clothing, but when you looked at her, you knew you were looking at a woman with a capital W.

Agnor knew she would be popular with the men on the crew, even those who were quite a bit younger than she was. Perhaps especially with those who were younger than she was. He knew she could teach them all a thing or two about giving and receiving pleasure.

He hoped she'd have some success bringing shy Bettsua out of her shell. If Lilith couldn't befriend the tall girl, then no one could. Agnor smiled fondly to himself, looking forward to watching that relationship develop. He wanted to see Bettsua gain confidence in herself, and he thought this cruise might be just the thing. He was already devising tasks that she could try to stretch her wings a bit, as well as push her power to the next level.

This first part of their mission was going to be a shakedown cruise. The brand new ship needed to be put through its paces before they could go off on their first real mission. They would have to test all the systems and start to come together as a crew. The relationships they built now would be vital in their future missions as a scientific vessel with a hidden agenda of gathering information on their enemies in order to keep Council worlds safe.

Each member of his team had signed on to that mission and sworn their silence on the real nature of the vessel. They'd been evaluated by the highest levels of the Council even before they'd been told of their selection to man this ship, and Agnor had had to fight to get some of his choices through. Lilith and Bettsua, in particular. But he sensed they both would be key to his success in this new adventure.

# CHAPTER TWO

As the last of the bridge crew checked in, Agnor stood to take a final inspection tour of the ship before they pushed off from the space station and started cruising on their own power. He gave Lilith responsibility for the bridge as soon as she arrived, nearly passing her in the hatch on his way out. She smiled and shook her head indulgently, used to his ways.

He took off down the hall, noting the shiny new nameplates affixed to each of the crew compartments. There were more compartments on this ship than on the *Circe*, and the lounge was bigger to accommodate the slightly larger crew. He took a lift down to what would have been the hold on the *Circe*, but on this ship was separated into several different areas. There were laboratories and a state-of-the-art medical facility that took up about half the hold. The rest was a cargo area that housed their supplies, with some empty space held in reserve should they need to take on any more cargo in their travels.

All of the stowage was accounted for meticulously, as it was on all space-going ships, since fuel and navigational calculations depended greatly on knowing the exact mass of the ship. Further, the way things were stowed in the hold was very important, since heavy equipment or supply crates could shift when the ship encountered gravitational fluctuations and cause untold problems. It would be Bettsua's job as Loadmaster of the *Calypso* to make sure the hold and its records were kept neat, orderly and safe.

Though she'd never been in charge of a ship's hold before, her recordkeeping skills were tight, and she had a lot of experience with inventory control in the job she'd held in the Council offices back on Geneth Mar. She'd had a clerical job that Agnor privately thought hadn't tested her full abilities, but she was painfully shy, and perhaps she hadn't wanted to put herself in position to gain attention and be promoted to one of the more visible jobs. He thought it was sad that so much potential had been held back because of her innate shyness, but he knew that was all about to change. At least if he had anything to say about it.

He stepped off the lift with a smile of determination on his face and made his way to the hold, bypassing the labs and med facility, for now. He knew Bettsua was on board, but she'd closeted herself in the hold, and he wanted to be sure she knew she was welcome on the bridge, since she held one of the key positions on his crew.

He found her frowning at a datapad she held in one hand while, with the other, she directed a huge crate of foodstuffs across the wide hold using her Talent. It was quite a sight. He stepped through the hatch and leaned back against the wall to watch, knowing she hadn't yet sensed his presence. He didn't want to startle her, lest their food go crashing to the deck, so he waited, watching with great interest as she used her enormous power to direct crates that weighed tons, even in the somewhat sub-standard artificial gravity of the hold, with a single offhanded thought of her Talented mind.

"This isn't right," she muttered as she let the last crate down and turned to frown down at her datapad.

"What's not right?" He pushed up from his leaning position against the wall, then walked forward, with what he hoped was a friendly smile on his face. He knew he'd startled her. She looked at him with wide, frightened eyes. "Bettsua, isn't it?" he asked, knowing damn well what her name was, but wanting to put her at ease with polite conversation. "I'm Agnor Dallesander."

"Yes, I know, Captain. I mean, Lord Agnor." She looked and sounded entirely too flustered for his peace of mind.

"Captain will do, if you want to be formal, but I'd prefer it if you'd just call me Agnor. And may I call you Bettsua?" He didn't quite know how to be charming, but he was trying his damnedest. This poor, frightened, shy girl was breaking his heart and testing his limits. He wasn't the most suave man in the galaxy, and he'd never quite cared before, but now he wished he had even a tenth of his old friend Darak's charm with the ladies.

She nodded at him, clutching the datapad to her heavily draped bosom. She wore the most unflattering clothing imaginable, but Agnor sensed there was more to this quiet woman than met the eye. He moved closer to her, reaching out with one hand to take the datapad from her trembling fingers. He had to practically peel it away from her chest and was pleasantly surprised to feel just a bit of warm, soft woman as he inserted his fingers between the datapad and what he discovered to be a temptingly hard nipple.

Not letting on that he'd noticed how tight her little bud was or that he'd just discovered how voluptuous her breasts must be, he stared down at the datapad, pretending to make sense of it. In reality, his senses were reeling. He hadn't been this turned on by a woman in more years than he could remember.

But he desperately didn't want to scare her off. She was painfully introverted, and he knew he had to tread lightly. Still, he couldn't help but be thankful that his Specitar's robes hid his raging hard-on for the most part.

"You can call me Bettsua, sir," she answered him softly, "or just Bet, if you prefer."

He smiled at her. "Drop the *sir*, Bet, and you have a deal. So, what's the problem here?" He pretended not to notice the very becoming flush of her very real embarrassment. She was really, really shy, he realized, even more than he'd suspected.

Given a question to concentrate on, she focused on the crates, and her eyes narrowed. "The manifest doesn't match what's here."

"Is there more or less here than what's listed?"

"More, captain. Those three crates," she indicated them, off to the far side of the wide hold, "have no records."

Agnor smiled and handed back her datapad. "Ah, I think I see the problem. Would you bring the farthest one here, please?"

She looked a little surprised and then went for the automated retrieval system, but he stopped her with a gentle hand on her arm.

"Come now, Bet, I know you can do it quicker with your Talent. I've seen you in action before. No reason to be shy now."

She eyed him for a moment before stiffening her lip in a way he found quite adorable and finally nodding. With a quick glance over at the crate he wanted, she had it moving through the air to land gently about three feet away from him.

"Beautifully done," he complimented her Talent, making her eyes widen. "That's quite a skill you have there."

She seemed too stunned to answer, and he smiled to himself. This poor girl was starved for a kind word. It made him sad to think that such Talent had been treated so poorly through her life, and he made a decision, then and there, that she wouldn't be so shabbily treated on his ship. He was captain now, and he would make sure she was treated right. Or else.

He moved the lid off the container, peering inside and smiling as he pulled back. "As I thought," he said, "this is top-secret stuff, Bet. That's why you have no record."

"But how can I stow it properly if I don't know what it is?"

"Ah, but you will know what it is, because I'm going to tell you. You are not to make any records of this, however. It will be your duty as Loadmaster to keep track of these items and have them available and ready for use should the need arise.

But without the use of any sort of written record." He smiled at her to put her at ease, but she still looked both confused and worried. "I know, it sounds fishy, but you'll understand in a moment. Come with me."

He motioned her to precede him out the hatch and then surprised both her and himself by taking her hand and guiding her down the corridor. They bypassed the med facility and the labs, coming to a nondescript portal strategically placed amidships on the underbelly of the cruiser. He pressed his palm on the keyed hatch, and it sprang open. Again, he politely motioned for her to precede him, and he crowded into the small space behind her.

"What is this?" she asked, looking around with wide eyes.

"It's a weapons station."

"Weapons? I thought this was a research vessel."

"Come now, they told you about our other purpose as well when you signed on, didn't they?"

"Information gathering…" she said softly, still taking in all the sophisticated equipment in the small room.

"Spying," he said succinctly, shocking her gaze up to his. "It can be a dangerous game, Bet. There are two other rooms like this one in other areas of the ship. When needed, you will deploy the contents of those three crates to these weapons stations."

"When needed?" she echoed, still somewhat shaken by the reality of what he was telling her.

"If and when we go into battle or need to defend ourselves."

"What's in those crates? Weapons?"

He nodded. "Ammunition. These stations are fully loaded now, but if we see action, those crates will be our only way of reloading until we reach Council space."

"Wow," she breathed. "I mean, I guess I knew we could be going into danger, but it wasn't quite real to me before."

"Do you want to go back down planetside? I don't want you afraid of the voyage to come. It will be somewhat dangerous, but it will also be one of discovery and freedom if

I can manage it. I won't knowingly take any of us into more danger than we can handle. I can promise you that."

"No," she answered quickly. "I want to stay. I trust you to keep us all safe."

Her eyes seemed to say more than that, however, and he found himself leaning forward in the tight quarters, wanting more than anything to learn what her mouth tasted like. He thought he saw the same yearning in her wide eyes, and he threw caution to the wind, moving the few inches more to capture her pretty mouth with his.

When she didn't pull away, but rather moved closer into him, he brought his arms around her, pressing her close. He realized with one small part of his brain that wasn't caught up in the amazing pleasure of her lips, that she was delightfully curvy under the voluminous tunic she wore. Her firm, full, voluptuous breasts pressed tightly to his chest as he plunged his tongue into her warm, wet mouth, and his hands easily spanned her waist, moving down to massage the cheeks of her tight ass.

She kissed like she wasn't used to the activity, and her shy response enchanted him. He gentled his possession, wanting to woo her response, wanting her to find the same mind-blowing pleasure he felt. He lowered his shields just the tiniest bit in order to see if he could sense any shift in her power. First joinings had to be closely monitored among those with Talent, which was one of his responsibilities as captain. Not that they were ready to take that step, but he knew his power was stronger than any other Specitars, and he didn't want to hurt her.

What he found when he lowered his shield just the tiniest bit blew his mind again. Her own Talent was a maelstrom of energy that swirled around his, teasing, tempting and pulling at his energies until they entwined and encircled them both. He'd never seen anything like it—except once before. Micah and his lady, Jeri, had such a meshing of their incredibly strong Talents, and they were now happily married and the two strongest Talents among the Council worlds.

He disengaged from her tempting lips, pulling back to stare at her in wonder.

"Do you feel that?" he asked, awe in his voice. The way their Talents were twining together was freakish.

She looked shaken, almost betrayed.

"I'm not a freak," she whispered before tearing out of his arms and running out the door.

He called after her but was stunned by the revelation of her ability to read his thoughts. *That* definitely hadn't been noted as one of her Talents on the last testing report in her file. But there was no doubt that she'd just picked up on his thoughts, unshielded as they were. It gave him hope that perhaps she couldn't read him when he was shielding normally, but still, he knew such a Talent could be hard to deal with. No wonder the poor woman was so reserved. It must be hell to hear every thought running through people's minds, especially the unkind thoughts that he guessed must be sent her way by people who never would say mean things to her face.

He went after her and found her in the hold, crying.

Not hesitating now that he'd held her in his arms and wanted her back there, he went up to her, shielding tightly, and took her softly into his embrace. She felt so right, he thought absently as he sought some way to explain.

"It was a bad word choice, that's all. I didn't think you were a freak. I thought the way our energies were meshing was freakish. There's a big difference, Bet. I've never seen such an immediate and intimate twining of two Talents before. You can slap my face if you want. I deserve it for hurting you, sweetheart. It hardly matters that I didn't mean to."

She stilled, moving around in his arms to look at him through tear-filled eyes.

"Why are you being so kind to me?" She looked so suspicious he wanted to laugh.

"Why wouldn't I be kind to you?" he countered. "You're bright, pretty, Talented, and you kiss like a dream." He winked at her, making her blush. "And I'm betting you're hiding a superior ability behind your quiet exterior."

She sighed in defeat. "They said you were different," she said quietly. "I should've known I wouldn't be able to hide anything from you."

"Isn't that the other way around?" He arched one eyebrow at her in challenge.

She blushed to the roots of her hair. "I can't read you, Lord Agnor. Not normally, anyway. Your shielding is too strong. That's why I wanted to come on this trip. I figured being around fewer people, most with strong Talents that should be well shielded, might be a bit of a break for me."

He considered her words a moment, then pulled her back into his arms, stroking her hair comfortingly. "How long has this been a problem for you, sweet?"

"The past few years, it's gotten worse," she admitted after a moment. "At first, I could only read neutrals and lower-level Talents, but now, even some of the Mages' thoughts are breaking through."

He sighed, imagining the pain she must have been put through.

"You need stronger shields yourself, Bet. I can help you there, I think."

Her wide eyes looked hopefully up at him, and he couldn't resist leaning slightly down to plant a quick kiss on her lips.

"You'd really teach me?" she whispered when he pulled back.

"Well, I can't let you go on like this, can I?" He smiled to soften his words, stroking her hair because he simply couldn't help himself. "Come to my cabin after shift change. We'll start right away. The sooner you can block out other people's thoughts, the more comfortable you'll be."

"Thank you, Captain." Her eyes filled with hope and something like hero worship that made him slightly uncomfortable. He released her and walked toward the doorway.

"Call me Agnor or even Ag, if you prefer. A few of my

close friends call me that. It would please me if you would too." He stopped just inside the hatch, turning slightly to regard her with one raised eyebrow. "You know, this little skill of yours could come in handy on our mission, Bet. Have you ever given any thought to putting your mind-reading Talent to use for the good of the Council? We have precious few people who can do what apparently comes to you naturally."

"I didn't know there were any others who have this miserable gift." Her voice was soft with discovery.

"Oh there are a few, but I've met none so strong that they could read Mages. And we tend to keep their identities under tight wraps, so that they can be sent out to gather information safely and secretly."

"They're spies?"

Agnor smiled cunningly. "Something like that. They do what this ship is tasked to do, just on a more intimate scale. They gather information that helps the Council keep the worlds and peoples under our protection safe. It's a noble cause. Think about it."

# CHAPTER THREE

Agnor's mind reeled with the new discoveries he'd made about shy little Bettsua Malkin. Of course, she wasn't really *little*—though compared to his own taller-than-average stature, she was still shorter than him. She wore voluminous clothing, but underneath, he'd felt a svelte, soft woman with generous breasts and sleek muscles everywhere else. He never would have imagined that.

Now that he knew what she hid under her sorry clothing, he feared there was no going back. He wanted her. Had wanted her almost from the first moment he'd seen her, if he was honest with himself. But now that he'd kissed her and gotten a taste of the way their Talents meshed so intimately, he knew he needed her in his bed. He needed to be inside her soft, welcoming, womanly body.

But how to get there?

She was painfully shy. True, she'd been more open with him than he'd ever imagined she'd be, but he figured that was mostly because he had taken her by storm and found out her secrets in amazingly fast progression. He had even kissed her while she was still in a daze, but it had seemed so natural and felt so right. He couldn't regret rushing her.

She called to him in a way he had never before experienced. He'd been with many women in his time—tall, short, thin, voluptuous, outgoing, reticent, and some who had Talents that complemented his own in enticing ways—but there was something incredibly special about Bettsua. He couldn't put his finger on exactly what it was.

Every time he saw her, he was intrigued. He'd been captivated on sight and his enthrallment had only grown the more he got to know about her and the more he was in her presence. There was something indefinable about her that spoke to him on a primitive level he had never accessed before.

Agnor didn't know what it meant. He only knew that he was beyond intrigued by the Talented Loadmaster. He wanted to know everything about her. He wanted to entice her out of her shell, and into his arms, and then he wanted to test her boundaries and encourage her to be all that he sensed was hiding behind her timid outer display.

He was virtually certain there was more to Bettsua Malkin than met the eye. And he wanted very much to be the man who helped her lay claim to everything she could be, if she'd just give herself the chance.

He made his way back up to the bridge, bypassing the labs and med facility for a later inspection. He had a lot of work to do before shift change in seven hours, but the time couldn't go fast enough before he had her in his chambers. All to himself.

\* \* \*

Finally, it was time to launch. Agnor had been looking forward to this moment since the day he'd been given his own command. He'd been torn about leaving the *Circe* behind for the *Calypso*, but now that he'd gotten a chance to know his new ship through the building phase, he couldn't wait to see what it could do in space.

It felt good to be the one giving the orders now, instead of one of many taking them. He liked being master of his own destiny on this state-of-the-art vessel. He had a feeling his enjoyment would only grow as he and the *Calypso* grew together, out there, among the stars.

Push back from the station went well. Agnor knew his chosen pilot was one of the very best, and he left the small maneuvers to her expertise while he checked status reports on his command console. He relaxed a little when the navigator gave their pilot the course, and they settled in for a two-day journey through jumpspace that would lead them to a relatively empty quadrant where they could really try out the paces of their new ship.

Once the course was laid in and the ship successfully jumped, he called all but the pilot to a meeting in the ship's lounge. Normally, the ship could've been left completely unattended on its journey through jumpspace, but the *Calypso* was still new and somewhat untried, so he decided to leave at least one person on the bridge, just in case there were problems.

A low hum of conversation greeted Agnor when he entered the lounge with the last of the bridge crew. He looked around briefly at the assembled team, noting Bet's quiet presence in one far corner with an inward grin of satisfaction. He just felt happy inside, seeing her face. He didn't think to question why, at the moment, but the reaction felt good and right.

"Thank you all for coming."

He motioned them to sit on the various surfaces. There weren't enough chairs for them all to sit at once, but several made do by hoisting themselves up onto the game tables. It was an informal atmosphere that Agnor truly appreciated. He wanted these people to feel comfortable with him and with each other, and formality would be the first thing he would see broken down a little.

"I've met most of you personally, but for those I haven't yet had the pleasure of encountering, I am Agnor Dallesander." He purposely left off the various titles of respect and station that could be attributed to him. These people knew full well just who and what he was without him reminding them and possibly driving a wedge between them from the outset.

"Before we go any further, I wish to make a request of you all. Since my recent, rather jarring elevation in power, I've become somewhat sensitive to the Talents of others. I would appreciate it if everyone would keep a tight shield around themselves for the time being, until we get more comfortable with each other." In reality, he had no such problem, but it was the only excuse he could think of to try to help shield Bet from everyone else's thoughts. If he'd been a multi-Talent, he could have possibly thrown his own shield around her, but being a Specitar meant he had certain limitations.

"It will be good exercise for us all, I think," he said with a smile, "since where we may go in our travels, tight shielding will be the norm rather than the exception."

Immediately, he felt a surge of power through the small room as those within put up an extra layer of shielding that he could almost feel tingling along his spine. He wasn't a multi-Talent like many of the people here, but with his new rise in power, he'd gained some sensitivity to others' use of Talent that was new and quite helpful to him in his work.

His eyes casually went over to Bet, and he was gladdened to see the slight lift in her shoulders as some of the pressure was taken off her. He had to get to work with her right away on increasing her own shielding. He hated to see her suffer for any reason.

"Thank you, that's much better. Now to business."

He went over the rules of the ship and his own preferences on how he wanted things to run. He also asked each section head to speak a bit, as well as each member of the bridge crew. They were his staff, and they would hold the greatest responsibility for the safety of the people on this vessel. It was a bit more intricate than the *Circe*, since all that empty hold space was filled up on the *Calypso* with labs and med facilities and people to man them. He missed the simplicity and intimacy of the *Circe*, but he relished the new challenges this new ship would present him. It was an adventure for him, and one he never would have dreamed would come his way.

But with his rise in power had come more opportunities, and he was living life to its fullest now, taking a page from Darak and Micah's books and spreading his own wings a little. It felt good. And if sometimes he still felt a bit lonely—especially now that his friends and family from the *Circe* were far away—well, there were new people here to befriend and bond with, and he would try his best to make them part of his shipboard family as well.

\* \* \*

After the long first watch, Agnor retired from the bridge. He probably should have been tired, but instead, he was energized. He knew Bet would be meeting with him shortly in the privacy of his chambers, and just the thought of it made his blood sing in a way he hadn't quite expected.

Then again, he had felt all sorts of strange sensations where the lovely Loadmaster was concerned, since the day they'd met. He didn't understand it, but that was one of the questions he wanted to try to answer by getting closer to her. He needed to know why he reacted so strongly to her. And he desperately wanted to know if her reaction to him was anywhere near the same level of intensity.

If it was…well… He wasn't sure what would ultimately happen, but one thing he knew for sure. He wanted to find out what it would be like to share passion with her. He wanted to bed her and be with her in the most carnal sense. He wanted to slide deep into her and make her scream his name in pleasure.

But that would come. In time. For now, he had a role to play, and it was a familiar one to him—that of teacher.

He prepared the meditation chamber in his living space, lighting it dimly, enhancing the soothing atmosphere of his inner sanctum. It was very like the compartment that had been set aside for his use on the *Circe*, but a little bigger and filled with things he had brought from his home. It was a comforting space, with familiar furnishings. It was a place for him to do his daily mental exercises in peace and comfort.

He looked forward to seeing Bet in this setting. If there was one thing he could easily see she needed, it was calmness and peace. He could help train her mind to find that inner peace that he, himself, needed in order to function at the highest levels. It was something most Specitars—especially those of higher ranks and abilities—needed to master, in order to keep themselves in balance with their abilities.

The room had a sunken, circular inner area, carpeted in a dark plush that could be made to conform to the specifications of the user. If Agnor wished to lay down and sleep in his meditation chamber, it was as easy as ordering the floor covering to change according to his wishes. The circumference of the lower, central area was lined with pillows in dark, jewel hues, some big, some small, all comfortable.

Agnor had deliberately designed the area to serve multiple purposes. He would use it as a meditation area, but also as a retreat of sorts, away from the uniformity, and necessary functionality, of the rest of the ship. Being the captain gave him certain rights and privileges, and this room was the main indulgence he had taken in the specifications for his private quarters.

Most Specitars required such spaces to keep them functioning at peak efficiency. Unlike multi-Talents, Specitars needed to find balance within themselves frequently since their energies were directed solely in one or, at most two, directions. They had to ground themselves and take time out to meditate frequently. Comforting environs were important in such pursuits, and this space already felt like home to Agnor with so many of his personal possessions strewn about.

A little later than he would have expected, a timid chime sounded from the door of his ready room. He walked through to the smaller room, leaving the portal to the inner sanctum open so Bet would see the welcoming atmosphere waiting for their first lesson together.

Beyond the inner sanctum was Agnor's personal quarters, his bedroom and bathing chamber, all the separate parts comprising the larger-than-usual captain's suite. It was his home away from home. His small private apartment, which was a luxury afforded only to the captain of a vessel such as this. Agnor knew he was a lucky man to have landed such a prime post, and such an accommodating designer, willing to work with him to get his space set up to his exacting standards.

Agnor touched the panel to open the door, greeting Bet from behind his desk, hoping to lessen her fright at what was to come. He could tell she was nervous and feeling rather intimidated. It was written in the set of her shoulders and the paleness of her skin. The poor thing was afraid of him.

"Show me your best shield."

He could tell his direct order startled her. Good. Perhaps if he could get her to concentrate on the task at hand, rather than thinking about her fear, she would overcome it.

"It's not one of my skills, Lord Agnor. When I First Tested, I had little shielding capability. I'm just kinetic."

Agnor nodded, moving around his desk to close the space between them. "I understand the limitations of being a Specitar, but I believe you've evolved since First Test, haven't you? I looked up your file earlier. You gave no hint of this mindreading ability at all, but you did test out with just a little bit of shielding ability. Maybe that's changed too. Did you consider that?"

"I didn't think—" Bet looked startled once more. "I mean, I never could shield well. I just assumed that was still the case."

Agnor tilted his head as he considered her. "Perhaps not." He moved back toward the open hatch to his inner sanctum. "Come with me, Bet. I think you'll like my meditation chamber."

She followed him, and he was gratified to see her wide

eyes and the smile on her face. She was so innocently beautiful she took his breath away.

"This room is lovely."

He could hear the true appreciation in her voice along with a longing for the peaceful space he'd created for himself. It made him want to share it with her, though he'd never wanted such a thing before with anyone. Not even a fellow Specitar, who could fully appreciate the place.

"Have a seat. Before we do anything more, I want to re-test you. Will you trust me to do so?"

She gulped but nodded. "If you think it will help."

"I do. Knowing where you are now will help me gauge how best to go about teaching you. And just so you know," he turned to a side platform where he'd placed the items he'd need for the test, "I'll make no record of this test. I know you're uncomfortable with people knowing about your new power, and if things work out as I hope they will, we won't want any official record of your true abilities."

She nodded again, though the fear was returning a bit. He had to stop that. Agnor swooped down to where she was seated and placed a smacking kiss on her lips.

"Courage, little one." He smiled softly at her. "I won't hurt you. I want only to help you and protect you. Do you believe that? Can you feel the truth of my words?"

He held her gaze, speaking without words of the things in his heart. She seemed to understand. She nodded, and the fear in her wide eyes was replaced by something more tender and infinitely more fragile. It looked like hope.

# CHAPTER FOUR

Agnor sat back and began the process of testing her with the various geometric shapes he used for a base level before moving into the special realms of Talent that Specitars ruled. It was always a challenge to test another Specitar of differing Talent. It was easy enough to test or be tested by one with the same ability, but judging the strength of different Talents was always a tricky call. Still, Agnor was well experienced, and he easily recognized the huge jump Bet's power levels had taken in recent years.

After that, they spent the better part of an hour simply meditating, working on the mental discipline that would help her master her abilities. When he judged that she was in a calmer state of mind, he began teaching her about shielding and taking her through the first steps of building strong, self-repairing shields that would help her keep out the unwanted thoughts of others.

She was a quick study, and before their allotted time was up, Bet had rudimentary shields around herself. It would take time to master the new techniques he'd just taught her, but already she looked a little better.

"How's that feel?" he asked her as they stood in the outer chamber of his suite. "You look like some of the pressure has been lifted."

"It has," she said with a look of wonder. "I don't feel their minds pressing in on me as much now."

"It will take time to make these changes permanent and improve on the basic shields you've started today. We need to work on this everyday, if you have time."

"I'll make time," she said enthusiastically. "Thank you so much for helping me."

"It is my honor, but you know, there are others in the crew who would help you too, if you asked." He didn't like how isolated she was. He wanted her to become part of the family he was trying to shape among the crew. "There are many who are experts at shield building. Brennan has a secondary skill in shielding, and Elric has some telekinesis and other Talents, shielding among them. They would help you too, I'm sure."

Bet's expression grew shuttered.

"If you say so, sir." She looked down and started backing toward the hatch. "Thank you for taking time with me today. I'll check with the others you mentioned." Her tone said that, clearly, she would not do anything of the kind. Agnor frowned.

"I'm not dismissing you, Bet," he said, moving closer, almost stalking her. "I expect you here tomorrow at the same time to continue your lessons, but I do want you to make friends among the crew too." He moved right into her personal space. She looked at the floor. "Why does that bother you so much? They're nice people. They would welcome you." A thought occurred to him. "Or have you inadvertently heard things that make you think otherwise?" He didn't like that idea. No, not at all. "Tell me, Bet," he coaxed.

Finally, after some waiting, she answered.

"I know what they call me," she said in a small voice. "I'm not a mouse."

Agnor reached out with both hands and pulled her tight against his chest. He'd heard the nickname some of the crew had been using for her. It pained him to think it had hurt her feelings.

"I don't think it was meant in a mean way, but you do wear a lot of gray, Bet." He chuckled lightly, putting one knuckle under her chin to get her to look up at him. "And you're awfully quiet and stealthy." He was glad to see a little spark of humor enter her beautiful eyes. "And I think small, furry mice are kind of cute."

She laughed a little then, and it was like music to his ears.

"You're just being kind again."

"Is that so wrong?" He stroked her cheek with his long fingers. "I personally think you're very cute and cuddly, like a little soft mouse in your gray sweaters and fuzzy tunics, moving about in your quiet way. Don't take it so hard if other people think it too."

"They aren't thinking I'm cute and cuddly. They're thinking I'm sad and pathetic."

"But we both know you're not in the least bit sad or pathetic, sweetheart. Personally, I vote for cute and cuddly." His smile lit his eyes.

"Only a man as tall as you could think of me that way."

He laughed outright. "Why? Because you're so beautifully tall and slender?"

"Slender?" Her voice held disbelief.

"Well," he amended with a sharkish grin, "slender everywhere but where it really counts." He daringly moved his hands up to cup her generous breasts through the drab sweater she wore. "No, here, you're anything but slender. You're downright voluptuous."

She blushed bright red, and he chuckled low as he caressed her, slipping one hand under her sweater to touch her soft, warm skin beneath. His boldness was rewarded with a gasp as he felt her body quicken. He went a step further, pushing up the bulky sweater and rolling it over her head so he could see and touch her without it in the way.

In seconds, she was bare from the waist up. Her face flamed with blushes, but she didn't move away. Didn't try to stop him. No, she waited, breathless, for what he would do next. The thought set fire in his veins as he bent his head to kiss the curving slopes of her magnificent breasts.

"You're even more beautiful than I'd imagined." His words made her shiver as he whispered along her collarbone on his way downward. "I've thought about you like this, many times, Bet. Have you thought about me at all?"

She whimpered as he sucked one tight nipple into his mouth, her hands coming up seemingly of their own volition to hold his head closer. He loved the feel of her graceful fingers twining through his hair, and he increased the suction of his lips on her firm flesh.

Her nipple popped free as he drew back, sucking all the way, and he smiled at the picture she made. Her breast, wet with his saliva, her eyes closed in pleasure, her skin flushed with excitement. It was enough to make him come in his pants. But he restrained himself with great effort. He wanted to come inside her sweet body. And he would, he promised himself, if not today, then soon.

But she would decide when.

Her actions and reactions would guide him. So far, she was with him every step of the way, but when he pushed her for more, he'd watch carefully. He didn't want to hurt or rush her, but he doubted he could hold out very long. He'd have to move fast, but hopefully, it wouldn't be too fast. He could tell she wasn't very experienced, and he had to make allowances for that, no matter how hard it was on his own libido.

For now, he settled for just touching her, stroking her skin with his hands while he gentled her to his touch. They'd taken a big step forward today. It was enough for now.

"Do you realize your nascent shields held up nicely just now?" He smiled in approval, enjoying the startled expression on her face.

"They did!" She seemed amazed by her own new strength, her voice the merest whisper.

"You've got Talent aplenty. You just need to learn a few skills and make the shields stronger and automatic, then you'll be home free. I promise. And I'll help you with all of it, even if you never allow me the pleasure of touching you again." He reached for the bulk of her discarded sweater and draped it over her, removing temptation from his sight. "I mean that most sincerely, Bet. I will never pressure you in any way, and if I overstep and make you uncomfortable—captain or not—you have every right to stop me. That goes the same for anyone on this ship. Or anywhere, for that matter. Is that understood?"

She nodded shyly, clutching her sweater to her breasts.

"Good. Then this is what we're going to do. I'm going to teach you to build your shields. I'll also help you with the other aspects of your developing Talent, to hone your skills. I can also help facilitate interaction with the rest of the crew. I think, if you get to know them, you can make some good friends among those I hand-selected for this voyage. I don't want you spending all your time alone down there in the hold, all right?"

"If you say so, Captain, but I'm an outsider. Most of the others either knew each other from previous assignments or have already split off into small groups. And the things some of them were thinking whenever I was around made me very uncomfortable. Based on those overheard thoughts, I don't think any of them want to be my friend—or that I want them as friends either."

"Not all of them, surely?" Agnor wasn't willing to back down, but he had to tread lightly.

Bet shrugged. "Not all of them," she agreed grudgingly. "But one or two of the younger girls' thoughts were especially cutting. I don't want to be friends with them. Not if they can be that unkind."

Agnor nodded solemnly. "I thought I had thoroughly researched the character of everyone on this crew, but I didn't have someone with your gift to see through the fitness reports to the actual motivations and thoughts of the people in question. Your skill is something that could be very useful to the Council, even if you didn't want to be an active spy."

He watched her eyes widen as he brought up the topic again. He wanted to get her thinking about using her mind-reading Talent on behalf of their people. Her new skill was rare and should be used, but first, he had to teach her how to control it, and convince her to try to actively use it.

"Think about it," he counseled, deciding to leave it there for now.

He patted her luscious fanny, revealed now that the giant sweater was out of the way. She really was the most beautiful creature he'd ever known—inside and out.

"Now put on your mousey sweater, sweetheart, and get out of here before I tie you to my bed and won't let you leave." He gave her a growling smile and was charmed by her wide-eyed reaction.

He'd have to work on that. The woman didn't know how attractive she was. Her self-confidence was non-existent. Agnor would fix that too. He had his work cut out for him, but he hadn't been quite this eager for a new pupil in a very long time...if ever.

He vowed he would have her in his bed before too much longer. And he would make good on his promise to help her make friends among the crew. He would try to help her learn about pleasure from and with them as well. No Council Talent should be as repressed as Bet was. Talents needed the sexual release and energy generated by the act of love. It was as vital to them as breathing.

The fact that Bet had apparently done without to this point amazed Agnor. If she had such a strong Talent without the added benefits of sharing pleasure freely, then what would her power be like once she starting living the life she was meant to pursue as a Council Talent? Agnor looked forward to finding out.

And he very much feared that, once he had her in his bed, he might not want to ever let her go. But he'd deal with that if, and when, he got her to that point. It was going to be a wild ride, and he wasn't entirely certain of the outcome, but he'd enjoy it while it lasted. Bet was something special, and he wanted to remember every touch, every caress. Remember and relive—as often as humanly possible. He just had to get her to that point first.

\* \* \*

In the days that followed, Agnor worked on both of his objectives. First, was getting the ship in shape for the real mission they'd been deployed to achieve. Second, but not second in his heart, was the goal of helping Bet gain confidence and skill in her Talent, with the added benefit of kissing and touching her, giving them both pleasure.

She wasn't quite there yet, though he had gentled her to his touch. She didn't run away anymore or try to hide from him. She was blossoming before his eyes, but she still lacked the kind of easy confidence she should have had. With her level of power, she should have been much more stable emotionally, but the secondary ability to read minds had undermined her confidence.

Agnor was working to rebuild it. As her shields improved, so did her emotional state, though she still seemed to have spotty control over the mind-reading ability. They were working on it one night in his cabin when she broached a subject he didn't expect.

"Agnor, I have to apologize, but I picked up on something, and it has me a little worried," she admitted, biting her lip in a way that made him want to growl. *He* wanted to nibble on her lips—and other parts of her body.

"What is it? You know you can ask me anything." He'd established that rule early in their training relationship.

With Bet's level of Talent, once she gained some control, most minds would be completely open to her. Agnor didn't intend to even try to keep secrets from her. The simple fact was—hard as it was to explain logically—he trusted her.

"Well, I didn't mean to, but I heard some of your thoughts this morning…about our first real mission." There she went, biting that lip again. He was so tempted to lean over and join her, but he had to refrain. There would be time for that later.

"What did you see? And where were you when you picked up on these thoughts?" His curiosity was piqued. As far as he knew, she'd been in the hold all day, working.

"I was at my duty station, but I guess I was thinking about you." She cleared her throat self-consciously. "About the work we've been doing in the evenings on my shields," she clarified. "And I guess my thoughts turned to you, and suddenly, I was seeing blue stones and secret orders. Does the Council really know where the collective gets those crystals? And are we going there?"

"Yes, and yes," he answered simply, amazed that she'd been able to tune into his thoughts all the way from the cargo hold, simply by thinking about him. "I was working on the briefing I plan to give the crew. You probably picked up on that. Bet, I have to tell you. I'm really impressed."

"Then you're not angry with me? I truly didn't mean to eavesdrop on your thoughts. It just sort of happened."

She looked so worried he had to smile.

"No, sweetheart. I'm not angry. Like I said, I'm impressed. I know the strength of my own shields. That you were able to penetrate them with impunity says something significant about your Talent."

She blushed so becomingly he was sorely tempted to take her into his arms, but he had to let her come to him. He'd decided somewhere along this journey that he didn't want to be the seducer in this particular game. Certainly, he would do all he could to entice her into making the first move, but he wouldn't run roughshod over her sensibilities. When they made love, he wanted it to be because she had either thought it through and decided to come to him, or her instincts and desire for him overpowered her fear.

Either motivation was acceptable as far as he was concerned. He wasn't picky. He just had to be sure she came to him of her own volition. She was such a shy creature, and he never wanted to hurt her or coerce her—even inadvertently.

"So when are you going to tell the crew?" she asked quietly.

"Tomorrow. We've done just about all we can to make certain this ship is ready for anything. So far, the *Calypso* has performed beautifully and well within expected parameters. We're ready for action, so there's no use delaying. We have an important mission to complete."

"But despite the weapons you showed me, we're not a warship. So what can we do about those crystals?"

"You're exactly right. The *Calypso* is a science vessel, with enough teeth to be able to defend herself, if need be, but we're not going in looking for a fight. Our mission is to learn all we can about the planet, the mines, any inhabitants, and the crystal itself. If we can obtain samples for further study, so much the better, but we'll have to see what the situation is when we get there. The information on the planet Ipson is scarce at best. All we have is the name and the coordinates, and not much else to go on."

"Ipson," she repeated. "That's the name of the place we're going?"

"Yes," he verified. "Darak and Jana were able to obtain that information on my last voyage on the *Circe*, so I know it's good. I've trusted Darak with my life on more than one occasion. If he collected the intel, it's as good as gold."

"Or blue crystals." She smiled at him, and he felt himself responding to the small joke.

She really was the most adorable creature. Smart, funny and, when she wasn't being self-conscious, eminently capable. Gorgeous with immense power and brains too, she was the total package.

# CHAPTER FIVE

Agnor held the crew briefing the next main shift in the rec room. He'd timed it at the end of third shift and beginning of main, so that only the second shift crew would have to take time out to join them. The thirds were going off-duty, and the mains were coming on. He left a skeleton crew on the bridge and piped his talk over so they could hear it too.

He answered a few questions about the mission, but for the most part, his new crew was eager to get started. He liked their response. There was no fear that he could see. No dissention. This team was willing to take direction—as long as that direction led them forward, into glory. Or, as near as a science vessel could get to actual *glory*.

Agnor was happy with his crew's reaction and felt light as he dismissed them all to go about their business. He returned to the bridge and gave orders to set course. They were on their way toward Ipson within minutes.

It was the mission he'd been looking forward to since they first found out about Ipson. The planet where the power crystals came from had been a major discovery on that last mission with Darak and Jana. He'd sworn then that he would go there and learn all he could. The crystals were responsible, in part, for the enslavement of thousands of Talents in the collective. Agnor wanted to know its secrets, so he could free them, if at all possible.

If he could discover the secrets of the crystal, it would be the most important find of his life. And if he, or someone else, could use that knowledge to free those trapped in the collective, as Jana had been, it would be the best thing that had happened for Talents all across the galaxy, for hundreds of years.

Just because those Talents in the collective lived under a different government didn't mean that Talents on Council worlds didn't feel sympathy for them. Far from it. There had been a time on most planets where Talents had to struggle just to stay alive and not be hunted for their differences.

The Council had ended the exploitation and systematic execution of Talents on the worlds under their control, but there were still many places in the galaxy where Talents had to live in fear. The worst of these were in the collective. By far. For the collective didn't just try to eliminate Talents. No, the collective imprisoned Talents' minds and used their power for its own ends.

Psychic slavery of the very worst kind, perpetrated, somehow, by the crystals from Ipson.

Over the next few days, as they headed on a roundabout path toward the distant planet, Agnor worked with Bet as much as he could. They spent most of second shift together, in his meditation chamber, working on her shields, which were coming along nicely. He also worked on the attraction that was ever-present between them.

He would touch her lightly, but with meaning he hoped she understood. Little by little, he got the feeling she was growing to seek out his touches. That she wanted him as much as he wanted her. He still wouldn't press her, but he was just waiting for the day when she decided to take him up on his offer.

And then, one night, after they'd perfected her first level of shielding, she finally came to him.

"I can't believe how easy this is becoming," Bet said,

marveling at the way the shield felt, now that it had become second nature.

He'd been so patient with her while she worked on learning the skills, she had fallen a little in love with him both for his kindness and confidence in her. He'd gentled her to his touch to the point where she craved his hands on her body, caressing, guiding. Her thoughts had turned to making love with him time and time again. She wanted it. So badly. And she sensed he was waiting for her to make some kind of move.

"It will get even easier with time and practice, but you've already mastered the first level, and it should be much easier from here on out."

Was that pride she heard in his voice? Pride in her abilities? Nobody had ever spoken to her in that sort of tone, so she wasn't completely sure, but she thought just maybe, he was happy for her. The feeling of joy that swept over her made her bold.

Daring greatly, she put her arms around him, hugging him tight. "Thank you, Agnor," she whispered.

"I'm only too happy to have been able to help you." He pulled back slightly, and he looked deep into her eyes. "You're a very special woman, Bet."

She thought she saw some spark in his eyes. Some little flame that echoed the inferno in her own blood. Was he as attracted as she?

There was only one way to find out.

Taking a breath for courage, she reached upward to tangle her fingers in his hair. She pressed her body closer as she raised her lips, seeking his.

She kissed him with all the pent-up desire that raced through her veins and was thrilled when he met her lips with a fierceness of his own. She had initiated the kiss, but he took it over and turned it into something molten.

Bet was flying. Her body on fire. Weightless. Held only by the strong arms of the man she had come to admire—and yes, even love a bit more than she probably should. Her mind stopped thinking as their kiss spun into an infinity of passion.

"Oh, Bet. What you do to me," Agnor exclaimed softly as he broke the kiss but didn't let her go. His lips traced warm, moist patterns over her cheeks and down her throat as his hands caressed her body through her clothing.

Too much clothing. She wanted it gone. She wanted to feel his skin against hers. Made bold by passion, she began to tug at his robes, slipping them over his broad shoulders. He seemed to pick up on her desire and shrugged his outer robe down, letting it slide to the floor, pooling at his feet. Then his hands returned to her, tugging at the top she'd worn, lifting it up and over her head in a quick whoosh that left her gasping.

He met her gaze as he reached around to unfasten her bra, licking his lips in a way that made her insides clench as he unsealed the fasteners. She imagined his lips on her nipples and wanted it so badly in that moment, a little moan came, unbidden, from her throat. Agnor smiled.

"I like those little sounds you make. They're like a challenge, did you know?" He grinned as her eyes widened, and she shook her head, unable to speak. "Hearing them makes me want to try for more. Like, I wonder what it would take to make you scream my name in ecstasy?" he asked rhetorically as he lowered the bra straps and lifted the fabric away from her body.

She felt the gentle flow of air over her nipples and knew they were tightening as his eyes followed each and every movement. Then his fingers traced over her skin, soft at first, simply brushing over the most sensitive bits of skin before his touch turned a little more demanding. A little more real. Those fairy-light touches became solid caresses and gentle squeezes that made her moan again.

He smiled again as he lifted her in his strong arms, lowering her to the plushly carpeted floor. She went willingly, happy that her daring to kiss him had inspired this display of his passion. He wasn't rejecting her. Far from it. He seemed as invested as she was, which sent another little thrill through her body, even as he lowered his mouth to lick at her nipples.

She arched into his mouth, wanting more. So much more. Her fingers tangled in his hair, cradling his head as he nibbled and kissed his way over her breasts. She liked the way he handled her, rubbing her gently with his hands while his lips teased. She was fast reaching the point where she wanted to rip his clothes off and take charge.

The very thought made her gasp. Never had she wanted that before. Never with any other man. Only Agnor made her feel secure enough—hot enough—to want to truly ravish him. And maybe, he just might let her. The devil of an idea came to her, and she couldn't resist.

Pushing at his shoulders, she turned the tables on him. Oh, he was a large enough man that if he hadn't wanted to let her take charge, he could easily have stopped her from rolling him over and straddling his body. But Agnor's grin told her all she needed to know. He was happy to let her do as she willed, and that was something special in her experience.

She reached for his shirt, ripping it in her impatience as his arms tangled with hers. He seemed to want to keep his hands on her breasts, but she had an even more urgent need to get his shirt off. He laughed at the sound of tearing fabric, even as she gasped.

"I'm sorry!" she whispered, aghast that she'd torn his shirt.

"Don't be," he reassured her. "I'm not. In fact, I like this side of you, Bet. Rip my clothes off any time. Any time at all." He lifted up enough to pull the ruined shirt over his head and toss it away. "Now, unless you want me to return the favor and rip those nice pants of yours, you should probably get rid of them while I can still think clearly enough to ask."

"Really?"

Wonder filled her that Agnor would even think he'd get that close to losing control with her. She was the novice at this, not him. In all her imaginings of how this might go—if it ever happened—she'd never dared dream he'd could get as caught up in the moment as she.

He placed his hands on her ample hips, sliding his fingers under the waistband of her pants.

"Really," he replied, holding her gaze with only a hint of amusement in his eyes. "Off, Bet. Now. Before we go any further, and I can't think straight anymore."

Those words. That tone. Unaccountably, they made her grin. She felt more at ease with him, and with this new situation, than she had ever expected.

Lifting up a bit, she wrestled her pants and panties off, with his help. Though it felt as if his hands were more hindrance than help at key points. Still, the pants were flung away with wild abandon, and she loved the feel of Agnor's long-fingered hands caressing her skin.

She straddled his legs as he lay beneath her on the floor, her center open to his questing fingers. Sure enough, he placed one hand between her thighs, searching lightly through her folds until he found the little nub that cried out for his attention.

She let out a little sigh of appreciation as one of his fingers slid inside while his thumb caressed circles around her clit. Oh, yeah. That felt so darn good.

"You're so ready for me," he whispered, his eyes glowing with approval. "So wet."

She squirmed on his hand, loving the feel of his possession, even in this small way. She wanted so much more, but for now, this was the most amazing foreplay she'd ever experienced. Agnor was a gifted lover, just as she'd suspected.

"Do you want to come for me, Bet? Take the edge off? Let some of the energy build-up dissipate before we move on to bigger things?"

She heard the innuendo in his tone, and wanted to laugh at the double entendre, but her focus was too caught up in what he was doing with his fingers in her pussy. He'd added another, sliding both digits in a rhythm, first deep, then shallow, then bending just the tips of his fingers to reach a spot inside that sent her into orbit on each thrust, until she finally exploded.

She cried out as the climax hit, riding his hand

unashamedly as he coaxed a response from her body unlike any she had ever known. It was more intense. More fulfilling. More...everything. And all from what amounted to a hand job.

She couldn't wait to find out what it would feel like to have his cock inside her. Taking her. Pushing her to even greater heights.

Just the thought of it had her body warming again.

"I want you now, Agnor," she pleaded as he withdrew his fingers from her body, petting her as she came down from that first climax.

He met her gaze. "So soon?"

He didn't look convinced that she was ready. She had to make him understand how urgent her need was.

She reached down and grabbed his shoulders, leaning forward, pressing her chest to his, capturing his lips with hers. She kissed him with all the desperation that had built up over the past days. Since the very moment she'd stepped aboard, if truth be told. She'd admired Agnor from afar for a long time, and to have him pick her for his crew had been a dream come true. To be with him like this...well...it was the stuff of pure fantasy.

Fantasy come to life.

And she was going to wring every drop of pleasure from this experience. For it may never come again.

She pounced on him, trying to convince him of her ardor. She felt the fire in his response. He was certainly eager. She could feel the thick line of his cock between them, separated only by the fabric of his trousers.

She wanted them gone. Now.

Tearing away from their kiss, she reached for the closure of his pants, fumbling in her haste. He moved his hands downward to help, but she'd already achieved her goal. He sprang free, and she only took enough time to push his pants out of the way before seating herself on her prize.

"Mmmm." She couldn't help the low tone that began in her throat and worked its way out into the open. She loved the feel of him inside her. Just as she'd known she would.

But dreams couldn't really compare with the reality. He was so much…more. So warm and hard and…with her.

The sound seemed to galvanize him. He bucked his hips, lifting her up and rolling over so that she was beneath him. He was like a wild man after that, stroking deep and urging her to greater heights. He pumped rhythmically at first, slowly giving in to the frenzy that overtook them both as their bodies joined and their Talents meshed in the most mesmerizing way. They were one for that short space of time. A perfect union of spirit and flesh, straining toward ecstasy.

"Come with me, Bet." Agnor's voice was ragged with effort, low and sexy near her ear.

She could deny him nothing. Especially not the incredible climax that had built so swiftly and threatened to overtake her completely at any second.

She shouted his name as the passion exploded inside her, working its way through her skin, into her very soul. Agnor joined her in bliss, stiffening over her, his eyes closing as his head lifted, his neck extending as pleasure washed over and through them.

"Bet, Bet, my Bet," he whispered as they both came down from the most delicious orgasm she'd ever experienced.

Her Talent zinged through her veins, fully recharged and, in fact, stronger than it had been before they'd joined. It had been so long since she'd had sex with someone that she'd almost forgotten the reason Talented folks were so easy with their pleasures.

In the aftermath of orgasm, she was able to discern a definite recharge of her power. The sensation of being at full strength for the first time in a very long time almost made her giddy. Being with Agnor had been a dream come true, but this unexpected benefit could easily make her an addict.

Would he want to be with her again? She sent up a prayer that it might be so. For the sake of these delicious sensations, but also for the sake of the tender feelings he made her feel. He was so careful of her, so car*ing*. Even now, when the passion was done, he kept his arms around her, making her feel special. Almost cherished.

She hugged the feeling to her heart, wanting to remember it for all time. This moment was special. This man was special. By his actions, she had already fallen a little in love with him, even though she knew a long-term arrangement between them was impossible.

He was such an important man to their people. He was a StarLord. Captain of one of the newest and finest vessels in the fleet. He was so far above her lowly station, it would be laughable to anyone observing this from the outside.

No, she couldn't really expect more than this moment. He'd been kind to her. He'd shown her things about pleasure that she hadn't known, and he'd given of his time and skill to help her stabilize her Talent. He was a good man, and she would forever cherish this time with him.

She would take whatever he would give her and try to be content with that. She couldn't keep him, no matter what foolish dreams his words and tender touches evoked in her inexperienced heart. She vowed to live in the moment and enjoy every second of being with the most remarkable man she'd ever known.

He'd held her throughout the climax and its aftermath, while her body quaked with aftershocks and her hips moved almost involuntarily to squeeze the last little bit of sensation out of their joining. She knew he was experiencing the same lovely bliss that filled her limbs, and the same recharge of his own immense power.

She was afraid to speak. Afraid to break the perfection of the moment with words. But it seemed Agnor had no such compunction.

"You are beautiful in every way, Bet, and that was the most amazing experience of my life." His words sounded so serious. She looked up to meet his gaze, fearing she would see goodbye in his eyes now that he'd gotten a taste of her. But then he smiled. "How about we move this to the bedroom?"

He wanted more. This magical interlude was not at an end.

Going by his words, it was only beginning. Bet hugged that knowledge to her heart as they disengaged and got to their feet. Agnor surprised her by swooping down and lifting her into his arms.

She giggled as he carried her to the inner door that led to his bedroom. He paused to kiss her as he carried her across the threshold, and the look in his eyes stole her breath. Somehow…this moment seemed important. More important than she had ever expected.

And then reasoning was beyond her as the cycle of passion started again as Agnor placed her on his big bed. He was a master, and she was his willing pupil, willing to learn whatever he wanted to show her.

# CHAPTER SIX

Agnor was very pleased with himself, though he could have wished the first time Bet had come to him—on her own terms—had been in a softer setting. His knees bore the evidence of rug burn, and he very much feared her backside might, as well. But she wasn't complaining, his stoic little Specitar. She was the most amazing woman he had ever known.

He still couldn't quite believe he had taken her on the floor of his meditation chamber. There had been no time for finesse. No time to set the stage or act out some orderly, scripted scene of seduction.

No, it had been hot and hard. Fast and impatient. She had pushed at his shoulders and even ripped his clothes in her haste. He'd been a little gentler, never forgetting that she was more delicate.

Her aggression had surprised him in a completely satisfying way. She was hot for him, and the fact that she couldn't seem to wait to get her hands on his body had only pushed his own passions higher. Hence the quick, but supremely enjoyable, interlude on the floor. He would never forget it, as long as he lived.

And she hadn't seemed to mind the hard setting. In fact, she had stroked his cheek as he picked her up and carried her into his bedroom. He placed her on the bed with the utmost care, knowing they had just shared something incredibly special. He wanted to repeat the experience—slowly—under more controlled conditions, where he could enjoy every touch, every moment, and make the sensations last as long as possible.

He glanced at the chronometer. They had time. Hours yet, until both of them had to be on duty again.

Agnor stood to remove the last bits of his clothing that hadn't already been torn from his body by her eager hands. He smiled, remembering the tiger she had turned into, if only for those few moments. He wanted to see that tigress again. Often.

"Don't go," Bet said in a sleepy voice as he stood. Something inside him felt a primitive thrill.

"I'm not going anywhere," he reassured her. "And neither are you. Not 'til morning at the earliest. Okay?" He still wanted her willing participation in anything they did together. He didn't want to steamroll over her. She was so shy, he needed to be certain she was agreeing, not just accepting.

"All night?" She sounded adorably confused, leading Agnor to wonder just what kind of lovers had been in her past.

"Oh, yes, my dear. I want to savor you. I want to make it last." Naked now, he sat beside her. She blinked up at him. "I get the impression your past lovers have been rather vanilla in their tastes?"

"I'm not a virgin," she said, blushing. "But I guess you can tell I'm not very experienced with variety. I'm sorry if that's disappointing to you."

"Never," he was quick to state. He reached out, wanting to reassure her. "I think you'll like what I have to show you. And if there's anything you don't like, you just tell me, and we'll try something else, all right? I love the idea that I'll be your teacher in some of these things, but I suspect we'll learn together. You have as much to teach me about what you like as I can show you."

He began stroking her lovely breasts, knowing she was sensitive there. He felt a jolt of satisfaction as her breathing hitched and her gaze turned languorous. He lay beside her, turning her so he could kiss his way down her neck, stopping at her breasts for a good long while.

He maneuvered her over him so her nipples hung above him, just waiting for his tongue. And then, he gave her what he sensed she wanted—he sucked and nipped until she was squirming over him.

*"Like that?"* he 'pathed directly to her mind. He was calm enough—rational enough—now to use his Talent even while he made love to her. *"I know I do. You have a beautiful body, Bet."*

She moaned and writhed over him until he finally took pity and allowed her to settle on his hard cock, letting her set the pace of his invasion. She took him quickly.

*"Fast or slow, it's up to you, Bet,"* he 'pathed. *"Do you like the way I fill you? Do you like the feel of me inside you?"*

"Yes…" she whispered as she took him, slowing her pace as she seemed to draw out every sensation for them both.

What followed was a slower, but no less satisfying, climax after a long build-up. Bet was in charge of that orgasm, and the two that followed, but before morning, Agnor took over again, showing her the highest pinnacle of the encounter.

He invited her to share his bed every night thereafter, and much to his satisfaction, she did. Their days were filled with main shift duty and work, then a few hours spent working on her skills in his meditation chamber, dinner and then a long night of the best sex Agnor had ever known.

They went on like this for a few days, though they didn't speak much about their feelings. Agnor figured they'd talk about the emotional aspects of their growing relationship when Bet was ready. He still had the feeling that the slightest misunderstanding would scare her off, and that was the last thing he wanted.

\* \* \*

Glena Zimt was ranked at Alcotar, and unfortunately, she had very poor personal shielding. Even after Agnor had requested that everybody put up tighter shields, her thoughts still came through loud and clear to Bet whenever they came within a few hundred feet of each other. Glena was in one of the small storage areas just off the hold, getting some cleaning supplies for her gunnery station. Bet knew the exact task, though the other woman hadn't bothered to explain her presence in Bet's domain, because she could read every thought in her head without even trying.

She reached for the additional shielding Agnor had begun to teach her about, and to her immense surprise, it worked! Glena went about her task, and for a few moments, Bet was pleasantly free of the buzzing thoughts in the younger woman's mind.

But it only lasted until Glena came out of the small room, a bag of supplies in her hand. She turned to smile politely at Bet as she made her way out, and it was as if her thoughts were piercing Bet's brain, so focused they were.

*"Yeah, she's the Loadmaster all right. Although I can't imagine why the captain would want to shoot his load into her. He must be weirder than I thought."*

It was as if because the uncomplimentary thought was about her, it had extra power to penetrate even Bet's new shielding. But she couldn't let on that she'd heard the other woman's innermost thoughts. On the surface, the younger woman was polite, if a bit distant, and Bet didn't think she was mean enough to say such things directly to her face. For one thing, she had no motive. But Bet heard the cutting remarks anyway, and they hurt her.

The realization dawned that she was damaging Agnor's reputation with his crew by being seen with him. Apparently, everyone was well aware of where she'd been sleeping the last few shifts, and she began to wish she'd never let him near her. She could only harm him. Hanging around with her hurt his reputation and standing with this new crew, and she would never knowingly harm Agnor. Never.

She decided she would stay in her own compartment that sleep shift—and all the others thereafter. She sent a quick message to Agnor's compad that he would find when he finally retired for the night.

She couldn't face him. It was better this way. He could find another willing partner among the crew—someone who wouldn't make him look like a freak because he wanted to bed her. Someone who wouldn't raise eyebrows and questions among the rest of the crew. Someone normal.

* * *

When Agnor finally reached his cabin, he was disappointed that Bet wasn't already there. He wanted her so badly. But all he found was a blinking message light.

He read the terse message with disbelief. His first impulse was to 'path her. He would order her to come up to his cabin and explain herself.

Then saner thoughts prevailed. Bet was a shy woman, a woman who had been so reserved and withdrawn with him until just a few days ago. She was still shy and reserved with the rest of the crew, and she had that unpredictable talent for hearing the innermost thoughts of those around her. He knew the things people thought, that they would never speak aloud, sometimes cut her already low self-esteem to ribbons. He'd bet good credit that something had happened to make her want to run from him and hide. But he wouldn't let her do it.

He wanted her too much, and he wanted too much for her. He wanted her to continue to grow and blossom, not be forced back into her protective shell. He formed a plan as he left his quarters to go knock on her door, just down the long hall.

He knocked loud enough to be heard, but she refused to answer. He tried 'pathing her.

*"Sweetheart, let me in. I'm not going away, and I'm beginning to look pretty silly standing here in the hall."*

Wordlessly, the hatch slid open. She'd apparently activated it from her bedside console. She sat facing the small viewport, staring out into the deep black of space.

"Why didn't you keep our date, little mouse?" He pitched his voice as he came up behind her. He had to play this carefully. He didn't want to scare her off.

"You don't know what they think," she said vaguely, but Agnor was afraid he knew all too well what she meant.

"It doesn't matter what they think," he said calmly. "All that matters is what we think. What we feel. The rest of the crew—hells, the rest of the *galaxy*—can go hang for all I care."

She turned to him, her expression clearly upset. "You can't mean that. How are you supposed to lead a group of people who are doubting your sanity behind your back?"

"My sanity?" Agnor was surprised by her words. "Why in the world would they—"

"Because of me," she whispered, turning away once more. "Because you've been spending all your time with me. They don't understand why you'd waste time with someone like me. I'm hurting your reputation, Agnor, and I won't be the cause for that. I'll have to end our…our…association."

She couldn't seem to come up with a word to describe their relationship, and Agnor realized he'd waited too long to discuss the emotional aspect of their bond. Now, of course, anything he said on the matter would be suspect. He had to figure out a way to prove to her that she was wrong, without seeming to wheedle or suddenly come up with emotional words that would mean little because they wouldn't seem spontaneous. He'd timed everything wrong, and he was going to have to work to dig himself out of the hole.

"You're wrong, Bet, and I'm going to find a way to prove it to you." He sat beside her, placing one arm around her shoulders. "Do you trust me?"

She hesitated before answering. "I do trust you, but you don't know what I heard."

"I assume this is something you *over*heard because of your

special Talent, right?"

Slowly, she nodded. The fact that she hadn't pulled out of his loose embrace gave him hope.

"Who was it? Can you tell me that?" When she seemed reluctant to name names, he played his trump card. "As captain, I really do need to know if a member of my crew isn't loyal."

That seemed to make Bet pause. Finally, she spoke.

"It was Glena," Bet admitted in a small voice. "She was accessing the cleaning supplies during her shift and was near the hold. We crossed paths, and her shielding has never really been that good. Even when you asked everybody to tighten their shields, hers always leaked. I tried to block her out, but her thoughts—and they were mean things—were directed right at me like...like...missiles or something. I couldn't seem to help overhearing them."

Bet sounded contrite, as well as truly hurt. Agnor hugged her, hoping to ease some of her discomfort.

"That's all right," he almost crooned. "You're not responsible for her unkind thoughts. You can only be responsible for yourself, and if you were shielding and not actively trying to read her mind, then you have nothing to feel guilty about. She's the one who has the problem. Not you, sweetheart."

Agnor spent the next hour talking to her, doing his best to convince her that whatever she'd heard, it didn't matter. He would not abandon her because of a few petty thoughts by a junior crewman. He didn't dare put names to the feelings he expressed, lest she be suspicious of the timing of his declarations. But he did his best to make her feel secure in his regard and cared for. He also did his best to reassure her fledgling confidence.

She really was fragile when it came to relationships of any kind. She'd admitted she hadn't had much sexual experience, and he had to remember that in his dealings with her. He also got the impression that she didn't make friends easily. She was unlike any other woman he'd known. She was special.

Eventually, he coaxed his way into her bed, and they spent the rest of that night in her cramped quarters, enjoying the closeness of a smaller bunk. While she slept peacefully in his arms after several rounds of delicious lovemaking, Agnor made plans.

He had to help her gain the experiences that would shore up her confidence and let her fit in more with the crew. Despite her progress in other areas, he'd noticed how she spent most of her time either alone or with him. She didn't have friends on board, and she had admitted to finding it hard to make them.

He also sensed the rest of the crew's distance from her. They didn't seem to understand her, and they didn't seem to be brave enough to broach the invisible barrier she kept around herself where others were concerned. They didn't see the diamond in the rough under her bulky sweaters, or the quick wits behind the quiet manners.

Agnor would have to do something about that. He made plans, and the next morning, before he left her, he asked her to meet him in the crew lounge after main shift rather than in his suite. It was time to put his plans into action...

# CHAPTER SEVEN

Uncertainty shone in Bet's every movement as she joined Agnor in the crew lounge after their duty shift. There were others already gathered there, just hanging out, some snacking, some playing games. Others were engaged in more intimate activities.

Bet joined Agnor on one of the couches, and he put his arm around her. They watched the news vids for a few minutes until she relaxed into his hold as they sat side by side. When he caressed her breast, she shied away only a little bit before settling into his touch. And when he began undressing her as they kissed, she was with him all the way.

Shy little Bet—as he'd come to know over the past days—turned into a tigress when she was aroused. He was counting on the tigress to come out to play, and Agnor encouraged her at every turn.

When Bet clawed at his pants and freed his cock, he let her do as she willed. And when she moved to take him into her body, he let her have his way, though he knew it was time to put his plan into motion...

Agnor signaled Petris with a short telepathic message. Petris was Micah's cousin, and he'd been friends with Agnor for some time. Micah had introduced them, and they'd spent at least one memorable voyage on the *Circe* together, gathering information on the Wizard collective.

Agnor knew Petris had a good heart and a well-earned reputation for pleasing his sexual partners. Agnor thought he would be a good match for what he had planned, and Petris's broad smile as he approached them reassured Agnor he'd been thinking right.

"Do you want another cock? Now's your chance, sweetheart. I'll watch over your first joining, and make sure no one gets hurt."

She jumped a little when she saw Petris approach, but her body clenched on Agnor, and he knew she was excited by the idea. Bet seemed to consider for a long moment, and he sensed her inner battle between the longing to be just like everyone else and the need to keep herself protected from others who might hurt her feelings.

*"I'll guide you, little mouse. I'll see to it you're safe."* He sent his thoughts directly to her mind in an intimate whisper.

"You'll be with me?"

*"Always."*

She nibbled her lip, and he couldn't resist reaching up to replace her little teeth with his in a biting, teasing kiss.

"Well then, yes, I think so," she answered in a shy whisper. "I like Dominar Petris. He's never been unkind to me."

*"He'll be more than just not unkind. He's going to shoot you to the stars. I can guarantee it. And I'll help him."*

Agnor 'pathed to Petris, sending him private instructions for just how he wanted this first joining to go down. Luckily, Petris knew him well enough not to question Agnor's request and played along.

Agnor pulled out, though he remained under her as she rose onto her knees. Agnor's lips played with her breasts, neck, shoulders and mouth while she straddled him on her hands and knees. She was in a very vulnerable position, but he thought this first time might be easier for her if she could focus on him rather than the other man. All she had to do this time was feel. Agnor and Petris would make certain she felt nothing but pleasure.

Petris began by stroking her back, then down to her butt, squeezing gently. Bet shivered in Agnor's arms when Petris skimmed his fingers over the puffy lips of her sex.

*"What is he thinking?"* Agnor 'pathed to her.

Agnor knew he was taking a bit of a chance asking her to read Petris in this unguarded moment, but he thought he knew Petris well enough to guess what would be in his mind at such a time. If he was thinking anything near what Agnor guessed he was, then she definitely needed to hear it.

She smiled and shivered, her eyes going wide as she leaned down to lick at Agnor's ear.

"He's thinking…" She hesitated, clearly amazed by the thoughts she was sensing. "He's thinking how beautiful I am, and how stupid he was not to see it before. He likes my ass."

Her whispered words sent a flood of excitement to his dick, but he held back. This time was for her. She had to come first. She buried her face in his neck while he kissed what he could reach, smiling widely.

*"What did I tell you? You're a babe, Bet. Any red-blooded man will agree with me on that, seeing you this way."*

"He wishes you'd let me turn over so he could play with my breasts." She gasped as Agnor tugged on her nipples, just hard enough to make her squirm.

*"No way. Not this time. Your tits are mine until further notice, mouse. I saw them first."*

"You sound like a little boy who doesn't want to share his toys."

She giggled as Petris leaned forward, stroking her ticklish waist, then pushing his hands lower, two long fingers testing her wetness, pushing deep inside.

Agnor held her shoulders so he could lick her nipples, biting and holding them gently in his teeth.

*"My toys,"* he insisted.

His deliberately petulant tone made her laugh, the sound enchanting all those around them. She had a magical laugh that stilled everyone for a moment and had them looking to see what little fairy had joined them. Agnor growled against her excited skin.

*"You are an amazing woman, Bet. Don't ever believe otherwise. And if you don't believe me, listen to Petris's thoughts as he joins with you. I bet they're nothing but complimentary. And hot. You make me want to come, and I'm not even inside you yet."*

She shivered as Petris's hands moved expertly on her and in her, readying her for his dick. Agnor wanted it to last a long time for her, but at the same time, he knew first joinings were tricky. Talents often clashed when they first came together, the power enough to cause harm to one or both of the partners.

Which is why first joinings were closely monitored among those with higher levels of Talent. Someone of greater power watched over the two who were testing out the meshing of their Talents until it was clear they would be safe together.

As the observer this time, Agnor had to keep it together long enough to watch over them, lest a buildup of power hurt one or both. He sent the mental command to Petris and held Bet tightly by the shoulders, claiming her mouth as the other man claimed her pussy.

Petris slid home, long and hard, and Agnor felt every delighted shiver of her body, capturing her moan in his mouth. He watched over their energies carefully, instructing both with quick telepathic messages when to hold back or release their energies. He felt the meshing of their Talents.

It wasn't nearly the comfortable, made-for-each-other way his own energies meshed with Bet's, but it wasn't uncomfortable either, and after her first small orgasm, they were even more aligned. The greatest danger was over for now, though Petris's climax could bring on another crisis point. Agnor would hold Bet and watch them both carefully while his friend stroked her to completion.

Petris was skilled, to say the least, and he brought Bet two more climaxes before finding his own. His Talent flashed and fought only briefly with hers, then settled down around them. They would be able to join whenever they wished now, without fear of hurting each other. But strangely, that thought made Agnor want to growl.

It should have made him happy. He'd achieved his goal of broadening her friendships and alliances among the crew. But somehow, it didn't satisfy him. Only having her all to himself would do, even though that was something rather odd in the culture they'd been raised in. Among Talents, pleasure was shared freely with multiple partners. So why did he want Bet only for himself?

It was a question he'd have to ponder while he helped her overcome her shyness and fit in better with the rest of this new crew. That was key. If he wanted this crew to work as well together as the group he'd just left aboard the *Circe*, he'd have to encourage them all to share with each other. Friendship, stories of their pasts, and pleasure. It was a sure way to bond, and it was necessary for people of Talent, for renewal of their powers, and to keep them healthy and happy.

When Petris finally left her body, Agnor graciously allowed the other man to lift her up, turning her so he could bestow a kiss of thanks on her plump lips. Still, a little demon of jealousy bubbled up in Agnor's mind that was completely new and somewhat uncomfortable.

Agnor wasn't a jealous man. He'd never had a problem sharing pleasure with anyone before. But Bet was different somehow.

"Thank you, Bet. You are a beautiful woman. And your Talent is delicious and powerful. I feel like a new man." Petris was polite. Gallant even, though he smiled wickedly and winked at her as he left them.

Bet didn't know what to say. She'd never been as free with her body as her contemporaries. She'd always felt like the odd man out and hadn't shared pleasure with anyone in a long time. But Agnor had changed all that.

He'd encouraged her. He'd made her feel beautiful and desirable, and he'd shown her that others could feel the same way about her. He'd helped her at every turn, and she would have been forever grateful to him for that, aside from the fact that she was wildly attracted to him and halfway in love with him.

She turned to Agnor, kissing him soundly, a wide smile on her face.

"You're the best, Ag."

She dared to whisper his nickname, knowing no one else could hear her. She felt the delight in him as she wrapped her arms around him as he shifted, sitting up with her on his lap. She nipped his chin and sucked on his neck, stroking his shoulders with his hands.

Energy was zinging through her. It wasn't the topped-up, deliciously full feeling she got after a night spent in Agnor's arms, but the way Petris's Talent had brushed against hers definitely gave her a better understanding of why Talents often sought multiple bed partners.

The recharge she got from being with Petris was very nice and quite a different flavor than the energy she had experienced after joining with Agnor, but it wasn't as powerful or fulfilling. She wondered if normal people with Talent went searching for something like what she had with Agnor their whole lives, trying out different lovers, looking for something so perfect. It would explain a lot.

Things she had never really understood about her own culture were suddenly coming into focus. Agnor had taught her so much, even the things he hadn't been actively instructing her in were becoming clear. He was such a great man. She counted herself lucky to be with him, and judging by the stray thoughts of those gathered in the lounge, this little demonstration had gone a long way toward restoring his reputation—and giving her a better one, as well.

*"Did you plan all this?"* she dared to 'path to Agnor, initiating the silent conversation, which was something she hadn't done before with him.

Telepathy wasn't her strong suit, but it seemed easy with Ag. Everything seemed easy with him, she realized. It was natural to talk to him and even 'path to him. Natural to be in his arms and touch his handsome body.

*"What will you do if I say yes?"* he replied, a teasing tone in his thoughts.

*"Hmm."* She pretended to think about her reaction. *"I suppose I just might kiss you."* She put action to her thoughts.

It was brazen behavior, but she felt giddy with discovery and new knowledge. She felt joyful for the first time in a very long time. Then again, Agnor usually inspired such positive emotions in her. She shouldn't be surprised by her uncharacteristically forward behavior. He seemed to like it, and the thoughts swirling around her—the few that broke through her shielding—continued to be positive.

The others weren't thinking much about her and Agnor anymore though. Their thoughts faded out of her mind as they turned their attention to their own pursuits. The sharing of sex just wasn't the big deal to them as it had always been to her.

When she came up for air, having enjoyed initiating the kiss, Agnor's hands were in her hair and he was looking deep into her eyes. The energy of the stars swirled between them for a timeless moment while their bodies aligned.

*"I like it when you kiss me,"* he said silently while holding her gaze. The moment felt significant, and it made her dare further.

*"I like it when you take me,"* she whispered into his mind.

A smile lit his eyes as she continued to hold his gaze. She was glad her bold thoughts had pleased him. It made her feel warm inside...and, if she was being honest, their 'pathing was making her want him. Now. Always.

She shied away from that last thought, knowing she could never keep him. Not such an important man as Agnor. He was hers for now. And just for now. Anything longer-term was only a fairytale she had best not entertain.

*"Come into me now, Ag. I want you,"* she 'pathed, wanting to stop her traitorous thoughts with the sensations that would make her cease thinking coherently altogether.

He slid into her with practiced ease, allowing her no time

to catch her breath before he began the slow, stroking motion that would bring them both to ecstasy…eventually. She liked it when he made love to her with that lazy languor that made her think he was taking his time with her. Because maybe…just maybe…he cared for her. At least a little.

It was a secret wish of hers. Silly, really. But she couldn't help it. Agnor was the most amazing man she'd ever known. She'd thought that even before she'd made love to him for the first time. And the fact that he seemed to keep wanting to join with her had carved a little space in her heart out, just for him. He was in there now, and he'd never be released—even when this voyage was over.

She couldn't fool herself by thinking that he would want to keep their relationship going after their mission was complete. She wasn't even sure he'd want to be with her the next day. She was trying to just take this one step at a time and not build up any daydreams or fantasies around a man who was much too important for the likes of her.

Agnor was a rarity among Specitars. He was a hero. An adventurer.

Bet was a shy woman with lots of hang-ups. She was thankful to Agnor for taking her in hand and helping her sort out some of her issues. The improved shielding was a godsend, for just one example. But long-term? No, she wasn't the woman for him. He deserved someone equally as daring, as beautiful inside as out. Someone who could match him, not hold him forever back.

She wiped the sad thoughts from her mind as Agnor made love to her in the crew lounge. She'd never been such an exhibitionist before, though one of her previous encounters had been on a workers tram in the city, during rush hour. Some of those particular trams were known as *orgy trains* for just that reason.

She'd liked being watched then, and found she liked it even more now. Although the thoughts of the crew had turned to their own pleasures and pursuits, she was still aware that they were there, some of them watching while Agnor pumped into her. The mere thought of it sent her pleasure spiraling higher.

She opened her eyes when her thought scrambled, only to find the younger men watching her. One, in particular, kept his eyes on her breasts, bouncing as she and Agnor moved together. Her nipples tightened as the younger crewman touched his own dick, outlining his hardness through his thin shipsuit for her to see.

Daring greatly, Bet licked her lips, just to see what he'd do. She almost laughed when his cock jerked behind the fabric, and she exalted at discovery that she had at least some feminine wiles. She'd never felt as secure in her own body as she did in that moment. Agnor inside her, others appreciating her. She felt like a sex goddess. Like nothing could stop her.

A little drunk on the feeling, she rammed herself down onto Agnor's cock, speeding her way to climax. She came hard as he groaned his release, his face buried in her neck as she rode him, still sitting upright on the couch. Others were watching. She opened her eyes again to note that a few couples were even mirroring their movements. And that young man had his dick in his hands now, splashes of his own come all over his fingers. It looked a little bit like the orgy train all over again, only this time the people around her weren't strangers.

* * *

After that episode, the rest of the crew started to talk to her more often, and the few thoughts Bet caught from them were sort of warily interested. Most of the men's thoughts were complimentary, while the women were either envious that she somehow seemed to have snared the elusive StarLord who was their captain, or resentful.

Bet didn't mind that so much anymore. Her ongoing relationship with Agnor had done wonders for her self-confidence, and the training he continued to give her in how to hone her shields and control her Talent did the same. She was growing out of the mouse persona she had worn for so long. She'd even put away most of the ugly sweaters her aunt had made her pack and had the ship's fabricator to churn out a few more flattering tops.

She still wasn't a fashion plate. That sort of thing wasn't in her nature. But the clothing she'd had made was both functional and streamlined. For the first time, she had body confidence and didn't mind showing her form a bit. Agnor had done that. Agnor and all the admiring thoughts she picked up on, from time to time, from the other men on board.

She wasn't really interested in having sex with anyone other than Agnor. Outside of that one adventurous encounter, she hadn't sought any new lovers. Agnor was quite enough for her. He was inventive and amazing in bed...and out of it. They'd made love in many, varied positions and in many, varied places all around the ship, including all over his suite of rooms, the lift, and even her cargo hold.

She blushed to think of that last encounter when he'd deliberately sought out the weapons crates he'd shown to her on that first day. He'd claimed their passion might just set off the fireworks, as he put it, and dared her to scream so loud her voice rang through the hold.

She'd been on the receiving end of a few speculative looks as she left the cargo area and had to pass medical on her way off shift. They'd heard her screaming Agnor's name, and somehow, she found she really didn't mind. Well. That was interesting.

She'd gone from hiding in the shadows to fucking the ship's captain at her duty station and not caring who knew about it. Quite a journey from overzealous propriety to what she would have previously thought was shamelessness, in a very short time.

She couldn't bring herself to regret it. Agnor was the reason for all the big changes in her life. She was growing dangerously attached to him, though she knew any sort of ongoing relationship with him was impossible. She seemed to have caught his attention for right now, but Agnor had always fully participated in the full sexual life of a Council Specitar, by all accounts.

Bet dreaded the day he went to one of the other women on board.

But she wouldn't ruin today by worrying about tomorrow. That was her aunt's gig. Bet had learned a lot about living in the short time she'd been aboard the *Calypso*. She intended to learn even more and put it all into action. She was changing, and she thought it was for the better.

No longer would she be held back by the strictures of her aunt. The loveless relationship with her only living relative had warped her perceptions, and it had taken Agnor to truly drive that message home.

Oh, how he had driven that message home. With every caress, every stroke into her sensitive body...

She flushed as she thought of the way he made love to her. He was a considerate lover. Inventive and sensitive. She couldn't have asked for anything more from her first real relationship. She only hoped it lasted as long as it could, and that she wouldn't be utterly destroyed when it was over.

Firmly, she told herself to stop worrying about tomorrow. It would take care of itself, sure enough.

Hells, they might not even be around tomorrow. Bet knew, as well as the rest of the crew, that they would be passing the border into enemy space during the next shift. The collective probably wouldn't just let them waltz right up to their most secret planet with impunity.

Agnor had told the crew to expect resistance and to be prepared for anything.

# CHAPTER EIGHT

Of everyone in the crew, only Agnor had been in territory belonging to the collective before. He had hoped this foray behind enemy lines would be similar to the last mission he'd flown aboard the *Circe*, when they'd used the ship's stealth capabilities to orbit Mithrak for several days while Darak and Jana had gone down to the surface.

The *Circe* had been able to coast in and out of collective space with relative ease, but the *Claypso* was a markedly larger ship. It had more souls on board. More mass to have to hide.

It also had the very latest technology and stealth gear. Agnor had studied the specs himself before ever taking the ship out of the yard. He'd even had a chance to give input and make suggestions, more than a few of which had been incorporated into the design before the construction was finalized.

As a result, he probably knew this ship even better than he had the *Circe*. He thought it would be up to the task of inserting them behind enemy lines discreetly, but until they'd actually done it, everyone on board had been figuratively holding their breath.

Agnor sat in his command chair, monitoring the reports from each station. Comm was running silent. The stealth suite was up and running, functioning within optimal parameters. Nav was monitoring course and making slight corrections for outdated star maps, in conjunction with the pilot.

It was all hands on deck this shift while they accomplished the insertion into enemy territory. Later, once he was certain the stealth gear was working property, Agnor would let key personnel take sleep shifts, so most of his top people would be fresh if needed in an emergency situation.

"The new stealth tech is pretty amazing," his XO, Lilith, offered as she stood next to him.

"Yes," he agreed, turning from the screen he'd been reading. "I hoped it would be. It looked really good on paper, but this is the first time we've put it to real world conditions. So far, I'm pleased."

"Pleased enough to let half the bridge crew get a quick rest period in?" One of Lilith's main concerns as XO was the fitness of the crew, but she was also gifted with a strange form of foresight from time to time.

"Have you seen something?" Agnor asked quietly

"Not with my Talent," she was quick to assure him. "It's just mathematical probability at this point. The longer we keep everybody awake, the less sharp they'll be. And the longer we're behind enemy lines, the higher the probability that we'll be discovered and confronted. It makes sense to start the half-shift sleep periods now, so that we'll all get into a rhythm sooner."

"All right. Issue the order. If you're good to take the con, I'll go down for first shift."

"Sounds like a plan, Skipper," Lilith said cheerfully.

They exchanged places as Agnor spent a few moments conferring with the navigator about their course. As he'd expected, his competent staff was handling things, and he felt confident in taking a quick sleep period now, before things got any more interesting.

He hoped they wouldn't. Not until they reached Ipson, at least.

\* \* \*

They skated through enemy space for several days, using their stealth suite to its fullest capacity. They were able to take advantage of three seldom-used and poorly guarded jump points that brought them closer to Ipson on a roundabout course.

The crew was holding up well under the strain of the shortened shifts and enforced rest periods. They were all professionals, and most had served aboard combat ships before.

As they made their final approach—fully stealthed—toward Ipson, everyone was back on station. Nobody knew what they would encounter, and the whole ship was on alert.

"Looks like there's not much of a welcoming committee," Lilith observed as they both pored over the reports from each station.

"I had a feeling that might be the case," Agnor said. Lilith looked up at him sharply. "Well, if you had a top secret thing on which your entire power structure depended, would you make more of a target of it by placing obvious protections around its secret location, or would you try to keep that location secret as long as possible?"

"They took a risk, if they left this place completely unprotected," Lilith observed.

"Possibly," Agnor agreed. "But we don't know that it's completely unprotected. Just because there's nothing obvious in the system—no orbital gun emplacements or early warning satellites, garrisons of troops or armada of protective ships that we can discern—doesn't mean there's nothing there. Or that there might not be something formidable down on the surface of the planet."

He thought through his options. The safety of the ship had to come first, but they also had to take chances to complete this mission. He had to use every tool in his arsenal to further their cause, and he had a secret weapon nobody knew about but himself...and Bet.

"Brennin," Agnor named the man on the comm panel. "Please ask Bet to come up to the bridge."

He had deliberately made the request public. Agnor could have just as easily sent a telepathic message to his lover, asking her the same thing. But he wanted the bridge crew to realize Bet had more to offer as a member of the ship's crew. More to offer as a truly gifted Talent.

Agnor wasn't sure she could do what he was about to ask her to try, but there was no harm in making the effort. And if she did turn around and surprise them all, the outcome could be very beneficial to the successful completion of their mission.

Within a few minutes, Bet walked onto the bridge. Her gait held a bit of the hesitancy she must be feeling. Everyone knew they were making their approach to Ipson. Everyone was on high alert. Bet had been at her duty station in the cargo hold; though at the moment, there wasn't a lot for her to do down there.

If the ship came under fire, she might be called upon to deploy those extra ammunition crates, but for right now, she was free to help him with his little test. He motioned her over, and she came to him, questions in her gaze. He could put some of those questions to rest, at least. She had to be comfortable in order for this to work.

"I want you to try something for me, Specitar," he said formally for the benefit of the bridge crew, who were all watching from the corners of their eyes.

"What can I do for you, sir?" Bet answered immediately.

"I want you to the lower your shields and see what you can make of the planet below us."

They had taken up a position in orbit around Ipson. It was a very high orbit, but the sensors were already picking up a great deal of information about the surface of the planet. It would be a few minutes before the scans would complete, building an image of the planet's surface. Agnor wanted to use the time by trying something he had been thinking about since he discovered the true depth of Bet's secondary Talent.

Bet's eyes widened as she heard his request. "But—"

Agnor cut her off, though not unkindly. "I know you've never done anything like this before, but I think you might surprise yourself." Agnor shrugged, trying to adopt a casual attitude. "I could be totally wrong, but we won't know unless you are willing to try. Are you, Bet?" He met her gaze, trying to convey all the confidence he had in her abilities.

She didn't look totally convinced, but she shrugged and tried to put on a brave face. "I'm willing to give it a go, if you really want me to."

"I do," Agnor confirmed.

He stood and motioned for her to sit in his chair. He knew eyebrows were raised all over the bridge by his actions, but he didn't really care. Bet had to be comfortable if she was going to do this, and safe from falling to the deck if she got overwhelmed. His chair was the closest. It would do.

Bet looked at him uncertainly, but when he repeated the motion for her to sit, she complied. He stayed near to coach her through the experiment, but also because he just needed to be near her. This little woman had taken a big piece of his heart, and he didn't think he'd ever get it back. Not that he wanted it back. It was hers, well and truly, forevermore.

"When you're ready, Bet," he said softly, holding her gaze. When he saw the fear in her eyes, he reached out and took her hand, holding it gently while her breathing calmed.

She was doing one of the exercises he had taught her. Relaxation would follow, and soon after, she would begin the process of dropping her shields. And then... Then, they would see what could be seen.

If anything.

Agnor followed her progress, watching her closely as she slipped into an almost trance-like state. She was focusing within, working as he had taught her. For a moment, he was struck by how far she had come in such a short time. She really was a Talent of incredible aptitude.

He marveled again at how she had managed to hide her amazing increase in ability. That, in itself, was surprising, especially when you considered that, until her assignment to the *Calypso*, she had worked for the Mage council. She'd been surrounded by superior Talents day in and day out. Not one of them had noticed what she had been trying so hard to hide.

Agnor was just grateful he had spotted her abilities. He was even more grateful that she had been willing to let him teach her how to utilize them. She had only just begun learning how to control her wild Talent, but already, she was showing amazing promise.

Her hand tightened on his, and he focused on her startled expression.

"What is it, Bet? Are you all right?" he asked in an urgent whisper.

"He's waiting for you," she whispered back, still in a semi-trance. "He is lighting the beacon and knows that you will come. Oh, God, he sees me!" Panic filled her voice, and her grip tightened again.

"Shields up, Bet," he urged her. "Block it out. Come on, you can do it."

"Wait," she said, her grip easing the tiniest bit. "It's all right. He's not angry. He's sending greetings. To me...and to you. He's waiting for you, Agnor, though he doesn't know your name. He is asking me if the tall man is with me. Should I affirm?"

Well, tall was certainly a descriptor Agnor was used to. His above average height marked him as different on almost every planet that was part of the Council or in the collective. He considered quickly what to reveal to the mysterious mind Bet was in contact with.

"Tell him I'm here, and I will come," he decided. There was something about this contact that made him want to trust—at least this little bit.

"He says the way will be prepared. And he's asking if I could accompany you. No one else. He had planned for only one visitor and was going to let only you on the planet, but he says my mind intrigues him, and he wants to meet me too."

Agnor didn't liked the sound of that, but he would discuss it with her once she had her shields back in place. Until then, she might be vulnerable from the obviously powerful mind she had encountered on the planet below.

"End the contact, Bet. Put your shields back up," he instructed quietly. "Do it now."

Bet blinked a few times as she did as she was told and came out of the trance-like state. She looked up at him, wonder in her expression.

"What just happened?" he asked, concerned but trying not to let it show too much, lest he frighten her.

She smiled. "I opened my shields, like you asked, and went seeking. There are many minds down on the planet, but one in particular stood out. And when I tried listening in to his thoughts, he became aware of me. I've never had that happen before. Nobody ever knows when I hear their thoughts."

She was speaking in a soft tone that didn't carry much beyond the command chair. Though the rest of the bridge crew kept throwing intrigued glances toward her, few of them had even a small inkling about what she had just done. They didn't understand the miracle of her incredibly rare Talent.

"Agnor..." She seemed almost hesitant to say what was on her mind, but then she went on. "I don't think... I mean... It's possible that the entity I just encountered wasn't human." Agnor grew even more concerned. "I think... I think the mind was that of the crystal itself. I think it's self-aware. And I think it's more in control down on the planet than the collective is."

Agnor was blown away by the idea. Thoughts raced through his mind. Nobody on Geneth Mar had ever speculated, to his knowledge, that the crystal could be alive. But why not? Just because nobody on a Council world had ever encountered something like this before didn't mean it couldn't be possible.

"If it's alive, then why is it working for the collective? Is it evil?" he wondered aloud.

"I don't think so," Bet volunteered. "I got the impression

that its focus was strictly on the planet below. Maybe once the small pieces of crystal leave here, they lose the connection with the larger consciousness."

"An interesting theory," Agnor allowed. "But until I get down there, there's no way to know for sure. This could all be a very elaborate trap."

Bet clung to his arm. "I know that, but if you'd felt what I did… Agnor, I really want to go down there with you. I think we're on the brink of something here."

Now that kind of talk was familiar. Agnor looked up at his XO. Lilith might be able to shed some light on the future, if her Talent was kicking in.

Of all the crew assembled on the bridge, only Lilith had been in a position to be able to hear what transpired at Agnor's command chair. He trusted her implicitly and wanted her to know about Bet's uncommon ability.

"May the gods help us all, but I think she's right." Lilith looked at the screen that showed the planet Ipson in all its blue-hazed glory. There was an oxygen atmosphere down there shared by most of the inhabited worlds, but there was more… So much more. "There's something down there that I've never encountered before. It seeks a pure heart. It's been tricked before. It's wary now. I see you there, Agnor and Bet. No one else from our crew. Just you two."

"What happens if someone else goes, or joins us?" Agnor asked, knowing Lilith's particular Talent allowed her to see many probable outcomes in a split second.

Lilith shook her head. "Not good," was her curt answer, her eyes slightly unfocused as she looked into the near future. "Just you two. That path has the likeliest chance of success, though even that is not more than a fifty-fifty scenario. You must tread lightly with this entity," she cautioned. "And above all, you must be truthful. It will not tolerate more lies." Lilith shook her head, her Talent losing its grip on her attention as her gaze refocused. "That's all I can see. Sorry."

# CHAPTER NINE

Agnor left the ship in Lilith's capable hands while he and Bet took one of the small shuttlecraft down to the surface. The ship had the most advanced stealth technology, and so far it seemed to be working like a charm. The shuttle also had stealth properties, which Agnor used to their fullest extent on the descent.

During the time her shields had been down, Bet had received an image of where the entity—if that's what it really was—wanted them to land. All things considered, Agnor thought it was as good a place as any. And if this entity could be reasoned with, it might be better than most.

Whatever happened, this had been a high-risk mission from the get-go. Agnor had known from the moment the order was issued that he would have to take big risks in order to earn big rewards. Or die trying.

He knew his crew was behind him. None of them *wanted* to die, but they had all dedicated their careers, and their lives, to the Council. They would do as they were asked, simply because there was no one better qualified in all the Council worlds, to do what they had been sent here to do. They were a unique group of scientists, soldiers, Talents and thinkers.

While Agnor and Bet handled the away mission, the rest of the crew was busy aboard, using every sensor and observational technique at their disposal to make a full orbital study of the planet. They needed to learn all they could about this world. Even the smallest piece of data might prove to be vital in trying to end the collective's stranglehold on so many thousands of captive minds.

And it could all start right here, right now.

Agnor began the approach to land, feeling the weight of responsibility on his shoulders. What he did in the next few minutes could decide the fate of thousands, if not hundreds of thousands, of Talents who had been captured and subjugated by the collective. It was a heavy burden.

Agnor unexpectedly felt the light weight of Bet's hand on his shoulder.

"You can handle anything the universe puts in your path. I believe in you."

His thoughts must have been very strong to bleed through her strengthened shields, but he didn't mind that she'd overheard. He felt no awkwardness in sharing everything with her, which said something for his feelings. He only hoped that she could feel the same one day, but he was very careful to keep *that* thought under wraps. He wouldn't pressure her. Not ever.

Her soft words wormed their way into his heart. How long had it been since someone had spoken such uplifting words of faith in him? Probably not since his parents had helped him bring his plasticine volcano to his first primary school science fair.

"Thanks, Bet." He covered her hand with his and met her gaze, inspired to smile by her words. "I needed to hear that. Even if it's not entirely true."

"I believe it with all my heart. You are meant to be here in this place and time. You are meant to do whatever it is we're about to go do."

"You're a believer in fate now? You're going to have problems with Lilith and her probability calculations if you keep talking like that," he teased her as he put the shuttle on a landing vector.

"Sometimes you just gotta have faith," she replied, more confident than he had ever seen her.

He leaned in to kiss her quickly before turning back to the necessity of landing the shuttle. He had to bring it in delicately, both to hide their presence as much as possible and because he didn't know exactly what the ground was like.

They were inside a ring of mountains, landing on a small plateau that rose out of the inside of a vast crater. The geography was strange, indeed, and Agnor set the cameras on the shuttle to take both motion and still pictures on every frequency, beaming at least one feed directly up to the ship...just in case they didn't make it back to the *Calypso*.

The scientist in Agnor marveled at the geology. He'd never seen anything like it on all the worlds he'd visited. The ring of mountain peaks looked like a round circle of sharp teeth, reaching into the sky. Inside that ring were other formations, including several deep caverns and craters. The one they had been directed to had a little flat plateau of rock shooting upward from just inside the rim of the massive opening in the ground.

Agnor wasn't sure if these structures had been excavated or had occurred naturally. If the latter, this was a strange planet, indeed. If the former, he couldn't begin to estimate the time and manpower an arrangement like this would require.

There were no structures inside the massive ring of mountain peaks, though sensors had picked up small settlements elsewhere on the planet. Still, Agnor couldn't be sure if there were people around here anywhere or not. The sensors were not reliable this close to the surface. Massive amounts of power were zinging through the atmosphere. It messed with some of the sensor readings, but otherwise seemed harmless enough.

Agnor ran through the shut-down sequence for the shuttle's engines. They were committed now. Whatever was out there—wherever it was—would have to be dealt with. Making a quick getaway was possible, but not really all that quick now that he'd shut down the engines. If he'd wanted to leave someone inside, engines hot, he could have, but Lilith's vision of the probabilities said no.

They couldn't afford to overbalance the odds by adding another person to the away team, and leaving the engines hot showed a level of distrust, as well as acting as a beacon if any hostiles were searching for them. Better to shut down and have to restart later.

If there *was* a later.

"Well," he said as the engines stilled and the constant hum of them ceased altogether. "It's now or never."

"Shall I..." Bet asked hesitantly.

"I have to assume it knows we're here by now," Agnor reasoned. "Crack your shields just the tiniest bit. You're much closer now to the source. I don't want you to be overwhelmed...or worse, taken over. Remember, the crystal from this planet is routinely used by the collective to enslave thousands of Talented minds. We can't be sure that whoever you communicated with down here doesn't want to do the same to us."

Bet frowned. "Let him try," she muttered.

His little mouse had found her teeth over the past few weeks, and Agnor couldn't be more proud of her progress. He watched as she lowered her shields a bit. And then, she smiled.

"He says not to worry," she reported. "He doesn't want to control anyone. He only wants to live in harmony and bring harmony to others."

"Is harmony another word for the collective?" Agnor asked dubiously.

He had to keep his skepticism. This planet was too amazing, and he could easily be sidetracked by the wonder of it. He had to keep his mind on the mission and the very real dangers they were facing.

"It doesn't understand the word collective," Bet said, cocking her head to one side. "Not the way you mean it, anyway. It seeks to bring order. It doesn't seek to control."

"That's splitting hairs, isn't it?" Agnor muttered, but Bet held up one hand.

"It's sending a representative who will speak for it, since it seems we aren't fully understanding each other with me acting as intermediary, and it doesn't want to *take me over*, as you put it before, out of respect for our wishes." She had the attitude of someone listening. "The emissary comes." She blinked and looked up at him. "That's all. It withdrew its mind. It's got someone to speak for it, apparently. We've been invited outside to wait. Discussions will take place outside on the plateau."

Agnor didn't like being out of the ship, but as he'd thought before, they were committed to this course now. They had to see it through.

"I guess we're going outside then," he said with forced cheerfulness. He felt both eager and a little queasy.

Agnor had been on many away missions before, but this time, he had Bet with him. He wasn't a chauvinist or anything like that, but something inside him *needed* to protect her from all possible harm. The queasiness was due to worry for her safety, even as he felt deep pride in her abilities and courage.

"It's a shame it can't 'path," Agnor said, repeating something they'd discussed earlier.

Agnor was a high-level telepath. If he could have talked directly with the entity, it would have saved a great deal of drama, but he'd tried several times. It seemed only Bet's mind-reading Talent could pick up on the entity's thoughts, which was as odd a phenomenon as anything else they'd discovered about this planet so far.

The usual concepts didn't seem to apply here.

Agnor took Bet's hand as they walked to the hatch of the small ship. He kissed her just once before he hit the control that would lower the ramp. Whatever happened next, they were in this together.

The ramp lowered, and Bet got her first real look at another planet. This world was as alien as she could have hoped. It was like nothing she had ever seen in vids and storycubes. This place was completely unique, and fascinating.

Agnor held her hand as they walked down the ramp. At first, she thought they were completely alone on the plateau, and then, all of a sudden, they weren't. A mist rose in a ring around the ship that carefully mimicked the round edge of the plateau. When the mist dissipated, men were standing in a circle all around them. And all around the ship.

# CHAPTER TEN

Bet did her best to control her reaction. She was very proud that she didn't jump clear out of her skin.

Looking at the men, she noticed they were all wearing similar robes of deepest blue. Some had markings on the fabric, and on their faces and hands. Some glinted in the uncertain light of the crater, and she realized those glints were crystal facets—some sewn into the fabric of their robes, and some embedded into the skin of their bodies.

"That's just like Jana," she whispered, almost unaware that she had actually spoken aloud.

"Who is Jana?" The voice came to them from a mist that had gathered at the foot of their ramp. As the mist cleared, a triangle of men, in those same blue robes stood in front of them.

The men were all shorter than she and Agnor, and their skin was either ghostly pale or weathered and dark. It was as if some of them lived and worked on the surface, in the sun, and some spent the majority of their time below ground. Bet had seen miners before, and they all had a sort of pallor, but these men took it to the extreme.

"Jana is a woman who escaped the collective only when the control scepter she had been given shattered in her hands. Her mind had been enslaved for many years, but she fought her way free of their control, and though she almost died, she is now recovered. Relatively healthy and free of the collective for the first time in more than a decade, she is traveling the stars with her mate, who is my good friend."

"Why do you say she is like us?" another of the men in the central triangle formation asked of Bet.

"I don't know her personally, but everyone knows about the crystals. They're embedded in her skin. Just like some of you." Bet looked around at the flashing of crystal that could be seen here and there around the circle and in front of her.

"Have you seen this?" the first man asked directly of Agnor.

"I have," he answered in a solemn tone. "She has over one hundred shards of varying sizes permanently embedded in her skin. Some are as small as a sliver. And some are as large as my thumb." He held up his hand so they could see the size of his thumb.

A sort of impressed silence greeted his claim. Bet looked around, feeling uneasy.

"How is that you speak our language?" she asked.

"Ki bestows many gifts," the man answered mysteriously.

"Ki?" Bet repeated, puzzled.

"What you call crystal. It is known to us as Ki. Ki teaches and empowers. Ki enlightens and strengthens."

"Sadly, its power has also been used to enslave many Talented minds in the wider galaxy," Agnor said quietly.

The first man looked grim, as did his fellows. His mouth tightened into a compressed line.

"We welcomed you here to learn your truth," he said finally. "Ki demands information we have been unable to provide."

"I will do all in my power to provide the information you seek," Agnor promised.

"Good." The first man nodded. "Will you come with us to experience Ki?"

Agnor nodded. "It is what I have come here to do."

The group of men surrounded them as they walked in a

processional line off the plateau, following a winding path that led down into the bowels of the crater. Bet looked up a few times on the long journey, shocked to find she could just barely see the ship from a certain angle. They were traveling deceptively fast, though their walking pace seemed slow to her. Still, they were covering ground at a rapid rate.

As they moved downward, the light changed. It went from dim to dark and then dim again. Then, suddenly, the glow started to grow again in intensity. It was a blue-tinged illumination that grew as they moved along the bottom of the crater. At that point, they were moving into the ground itself, into a massive cavern that glowed brightly.

It was beautiful. Alien in the extreme, but amazingly lovely. Blue flickered along the walls of the long, narrow corridor that led...somewhere. The source of the light was there. Wherever this tall tunnel led.

Fear had been left far behind. This was an experience like no other, and Bet wasn't afraid. Somehow, Agnor's presence calmed and reassured her. She felt as if nothing bad could happen to her with him around, unreasonable as that seemed.

The line of men shuffled and reformed until they were walking single-file through the narrowest part of the tunnel. The light was growing brighter and moving now as they drew near to what appeared to be an opening. Agnor led, holding Bet's hand as he stepped through first. She followed and nearly tripped over her own feet.

They were in a massive underground chamber that danced with radiance in the blue part of the spectrum. The walls and parts of the floor of the cavern was filled with crystals of varying sizes, and the beams bounced from shard to shard, pillar to pillar. The play of light was both fascinating and inexplicable.

They were in an enclosed chamber. There should be no light source to illuminate the crystals in such a way. Unless...the light was coming from inside the crystals themselves.

Bet gradually became aware that the robed men filed in

behind her and arrayed themselves around the giant room. They all faced inward, forming a rough circle in the open spots of the floor, between the crystals. Some were so massive she wouldn't be able to get both arms around them. Some were tiny, as if they'd only just started growing. All danced with the blue glow that bounced around inside the crystal lattice and out into the world around.

Perhaps that was the way they communicated with each other, if they were all different entities. Or maybe, if it was one giant entity, that's the way information was passed from one part of the organism to another.

"Is this Ki?" Agnor asked aloud, stepping a pace forward into the chamber.

"Ki is here. Ki is all around." The main speaker had stayed near.

"I am Agnor, a scientist from a world called Geneth Mar, which is home to the Council."

Agnor tugged on Bet's hand, and she stepped closer, moving next to him. "And I'm Bettsua, also from Geneth Mar. I'm a Specitar, like Agnor, but my power is telekinesis."

"What does that mean?" the robed man asked.

"I can move things with my mind," she explained. Maybe these people used different terms for that Talent. But if the crystal was somehow translating or interpreting, why wasn't there an equivalent term?

"Can you demonstrate this power?" the man asked. Bet nodded, and he pointed to a plain rock—not one with crystal on it—near her feet. "Please lift that with your mind, to waist height."

She did as he asked and realized every eye in the room was on her. "What would you like me to do with it?"

The man started, shocked out of his reverie. "Please place it over there." He pointed to a clear spot about five feet away. Bet complied with his request and placed it neatly in the spot he'd asked for.

"Do you need to rest?" he asked solicitously.

"No, thank you. I'm fine. I lift more than that every day. It doesn't tire me. It's part of my job," she tried to explain. The men in the room looked impressed.

"And do you share this power, Agnor?" He spoke Agnor's name as if it came with difficulty to his tongue.

"No. I am a telepath. I speak mind-to-mind with others who have the same ability." Agnor seemed to realize these guys needed explanations. "I can speak to one or two minds that are strong enough, on nearby planets. When I'm on my homeworld, or any Council world, where such Talents are common, I can speak with many people who share this gift over vast distances."

"We are aware of such skills," the man confirmed. "But nobody on Ipson has such abilities. It is forbidden by Ki."

"Because of the way Ki influences such Talents," Agnor said quietly.

"Yes," the robed man answered quickly, with new respect.

"Then, may I ask why Ki allows the crystals to leave this world and go to the collective?" Agnor dared to ask the question burning in Bet's mind. "The blue crystals are used to enslave Talented minds so that only a small number of masters rule them all. The control scepters allow armadas to attack peaceful planets and claim them for the collective. And once under control of the collective, Talented children are stolen from their parents and forced into servitude, their Talents usurped by the masters. It is a horrible way to live and one that I believe no human being would seek, given the choice."

"Ki brings order, but for some time now, those of us who serve Ki have wondered about the representatives who come here, seeking Ki's favor. Their minds are blocked to Ki, and their words have begun to ring false with us, Ki's servants. We wish to know your truth, as you see it." He cleared his throat uncomfortably. "Ki would like to commune with your minds so that it may read the truth of your words for itself." The man looked uncomfortable. "This is something that is seldom, if ever, done, and among our folk, it leaves a person permanently changed…not for the better. But our minds are not like yours. You have powers that we cannot fully understand. Perhaps it will go better for you." He shrugged. "Either way, it is up to you. Ki cannot change paths if truth is not discovered."

"I'll take the risk," Agnor said almost at once. "The crystals are killing innocents. If I can convince Ki to stop allowing the collective to mine here, I would gladly forfeit whatever I have to."

"Wait." Bet almost hated to speak, but she knew her time had come to act. "You're too important, Agnor. This is something I can do. I've touched the mind of Ki before." She moved forward, stepping in front of Agnor.

She knew she had to move fast, before he could stop her. Taking a deep breath, Bet dropped her shields and allowed her mind to touch that alien entity she had made contact with once before. And...she was subsumed.

Agnor raced to catch her as she fell. Bet had collapsed, and if he hadn't been so close to her, he wouldn't have been able to grab her before she hit the ground. As it was, she'd landed in his arms—just barely. The robed men encircled them, but that was the least of Agnor's problems. He worried for Bet. She looked very pale.

He held her gently, worry riding him hard as the minutes dragged on. He knew she was communing with the alien entity and he didn't even want to consider the great risk she was taking. Each second was an agony for him as he waited for her to come out of it. To come back to him.

Would she be whole? Or would she be damaged in some way? Perhaps her psyche might even be damaged beyond repair. It didn't bear thinking about.

He held her, searching her face for some sign of waking, though her eyes were closed as if she was asleep. But he knew it wasn't a natural sleep state. For one thing, the usual background hum of her consciousness was...elsewhere...at the moment. He didn't really know what that meant, since it was something he'd never experienced before, but it added to his worry.

He didn't know how long the moment lasted. It could have been mere minutes, or it could have been the agonizing hours it felt like, but eventually, she stirred. Her consciousness returned from wherever it had been, and a few seconds later, her face twitched in a way he thought adorable. As if she'd been tickled in her sleep and was slightly annoyed by it. Slowly, she came back into her body and rose from whatever altered state she had gone into when she attempted to communicate with Ki.

Her eyes blinked open and focused slowly on him. Thank goodness.

"What happened?" she asked quietly.

"Ki has gained understanding," the spokesman for the robed men said from over Agnor's shoulder.

"What does that even mean?" Agnor looked over his shoulder at the man, his temper frayed by the possible damage done to Bet.

*"It means we can speak with you directly now,"* said a voice in Agnor's mind. A telepathic voice with a feel to it of vast power, tempered by will. *"We learned the way from your mate's mind. She has an orderly mind with great power. She will be fine. She was not harmed by our touch."*

Agnor rose from his crouching position, taking Bet with him. He steadied her for a moment, looking deep into her eyes, before finally letting go. She seemed no worse for the experience, though her energy levels were a little lower than they had been before. No doubt the experience of communicating with the crystal entity had taken some toll on her endurance, but given enough rest—and maybe a little special healing time spent in pleasure together as soon as they were alone again—he hoped she would recuperate quickly.

Bet stood on shaky legs, moving out of his embrace. She sent him a small smile that went a long way toward reassuring him. She seemed to get steadier with each passing moment, much to his relief.

"I'll be okay," she said, reassuring him. "You need to talk

with Ki."

There was a boulder behind her, and she leaned on it. He sent her a doubtful look, but she made a pushing gesture with her hands, as if she was pushing him toward the crystal entity, encouraging him to talk with it.

That was why he'd come here, after all. To learn all he could about the crystal. And here he was, closer to it than ever before, but he was torn. He wanted to be absolutely certain Bet was all right. Everything else—everyone else, in the entire universe—was secondary to her. And that thought gave him pause.

It was at that moment he knew for certain. She was his perfect match. His life mate. The only woman he would ever love and want to spend the rest of his life with... If she would have him.

He would spend the rest of his life convincing her, if he had to, but he had to get this mission done first. Then, he could devote all his energy to earning the love of his lady.

He turned back to the center of the vast crystal chamber. And then, he opened his mind...

# CHAPTER ELEVEN

Bet had no idea what passed between Agnor and Ki, but she understood a bit more about the crystal than she had before. It was, as they'd thought, alive. It had rummaged through her mind, examining her past, her thoughts, her experiences. It had *learned* her. And it seemed to have taken the parts it needed to understand how to 'path, though that wasn't one of Bet's true abilities.

Like most children on Council worlds, she had learned the basics of 'pathing in elementary school. All children were taught about all the various forms of Talent, since many would either grow up to be a multi-Talent or have friends who were. It was considered basic education to understand the way of it and to recognize its use in others.

Ki had been interested in those memories especially, and it had learned fast. Bet had little education in alien life forms. It wasn't one of her interests. Now, she wished she'd paid a bit more attention in those lectures. Something in them might've allowed her to understand what Ki was a little better.

Though, she felt confident she'd done her part. She'd facilitated the communication between Ki and Agnor. His was the bigger role here. Agnor was the diplomat, the scientist, the adventurer. He would do his part for Geneth Mar. He was the captain.

She was only a crew member. A cog in the beautiful, high-tech wheel that was the *Calypso*.

She sat on the rock and waited. She might have napped, she wasn't sure. Everything since dropping her shields to Ki was a little blurry and unreal.

She was aware of the robed men watching them with keen interest, though they made no moves to interfere with Agnor or herself. They observed, and one or two had frowns of what looked like concern on their faces.

She must have dozed off—or maybe even blacked out—because the next thing she knew, a woman, wearing the same robes as the men, but in a lighter color, touched her arm. She must have shaken Bet awake.

Agnor was still standing where she'd last seen him, but the number of men in the chamber had thinned considerably. They were still stationed around the huge room in a loose circle formed around Agnor, but there were less of them.

"Lady, will you come with me? I have laid out refreshments. Your man will be some time talking with Ki, and you should be comfortable."

The woman had a tiny sliver of the crystal embedded between her eyebrows. It glistened in the sparkling light of the crystal chamber.

"I'm not sure I should leave Agnor…" Bet began, but the woman smiled and pointed toward a fissure in the rock, similar to the one they'd walked down to get here. It was another tunnel.

"We are only going into the antechamber that is five meters beyond this cavern. It is often used as a retiring room where priests can eat and drink between duties. You will not be far, and you can see your man from the opening. There is a chair positioned just for that purpose, so that one priest knows when to take over from the last."

Bet looked from the opening to Agnor and back again. She was torn. She didn't want to leave him, and trusting these people was hard. She had only this strange woman's word. It could be some sort of trap. Maybe they wanted to separate her from Agnor for some sinister reason.

And Bet couldn't let down her shields here. Not with the power of the crystal so close. She would probably black out again, which would leave her in an even worse position.

"My name is Lara," the woman said, smiling again. "I am a priestess of Ki. All the men you have seen here are Ki's priests, as well, of differing ranks and experiences. Ki signaled us all to come on this most momentous of days. Ki would want you to be comfortable while you wait. Ki's understanding of time is not the same as ours. That's why there are so many of us."

"How does that work?" Bet asked quietly. She didn't really understand what the woman was driving at.

"Come with me, and I will explain more, where we can talk without the possibility of disturbing them." Lara gestured toward Agnor. He hadn't moved. He was still communing with Ki. "The priests will watch over your man and intervene if he seems to be in distress."

"Is that likely?" Bet got up and walked slowly toward the opening in the rock the woman had indicated. She kept one eye on Agnor, worried for him.

"If he were like us, then yes, it is probable. But we've already seen that you are both different. You have what Ki calls *orderly minds*. Ki is best able to communicate with that kind of mind, but also determined that nobody of that kind should live on this planet or serve as a priest."

"That seems..." Bet thought about it for a moment, and finally realized what a few Talented minds in the collective had managed to do with little pieces of this crystal. "Oh. I see."

Lara smiled softly. "Ki has only communicated with one other mind like yours in the time I have served as a priestess. A blue-skinned man. We all took his coloration to mean something special, since Ki is also that particular shade of blue."

"Everyone from Liata is blue-skinned," Bet said, thinking aloud as she sat on the stone bench where she could still keep

Agnor in sight.

"So it wasn't a sign? There is a whole world of people that color?" Lara asked uncertainly.

Bet nodded. "Liata is an agricultural world with a unique sun. I believe something in the spectrum of light emitted by its sun caused the people there to develop a blue coloration. They are all various shades of blue, from what I've heard. I've only seen a few Liatans in person. Most seem to stay on their homeworld. From what I hear, it's a lovely place, though the collective tried to invade a while back and managed to inflict a lot of damage on the surface."

"What is the collective?" Lara looked suspicious.

"Agnor and I...we come from a group of worlds ruled by the Council. It is a form of government where a large group of Talented people rule as a group. The Council makes laws and policy for all the worlds under Council control. Our biggest enemy is the collective." Bet wondered how much she should say and decided honesty was the best policy since it was likely that Ki already had seen everything in her mind already. "The collective is ever-expanding and frequently attacks Council worlds, trying to take over. Every few years, there's a different incursion and many Council citizens are either killed or captured if the invasion isn't stopped in space."

"That sounds awful," Lara murmured, giving Bet a mug filled with what looked and smelled like some kind of sweet fruit juice. "What do they do with the captives?"

"The collective imprisons any Talented mind and steals their power. The non-Talented citizens are mostly left alone, though they have to adhere to collective laws and policies—which includes a yearly tithe of people. Young Talents are taken away from their families, and their minds trapped. Others are taken for the collective's vast army."

"They steal children from their families?" Lara frowned.

"Sadly, yes. I know for a fact that Agnor's friend, Jana, was stolen from her family when she was just a teenager. Her parents were murdered, and her sister, Jeri, ran away, evading capture. When the collective invaded Liata, Jana was leading the armada. She was completely under the control of the collective's puppet masters."

"How does that work? Did she not realize what she was doing?" Lara asked.

"The collective doesn't allow independent thought among those minds it imprisons and uses. Only a few minds are free in the collective, and they direct the rest. Jana testified before the Council that she heard what she called the Voice of the collective in her mind at all times and was only free of it at short intervals."

"That's..." Lara seemed at a loss for words.

"Yeah, it's pretty terrible," Bet agreed.

"Ki brings order, but if it is not by choice, it is a grave misuse of Ki's innate power. We know this is the will of Ki. We know some of the dangers Ki can be for unprotected minds. Your minds. Not ours. We don't have the right kind of order for Ki's power, which makes it both harder, and safer, for us to serve."

"Well, we came here because Jana discovered where the collective had been obtaining the crystal. She had a control scepter in her hand when the armada she was leading in attack on Liata exploded. Jana now has many splinters of that crystal embedded in her skin, and her mind is finally free of the collective's control."

"Why didn't she come here herself?" Lara wanted to know.

"Jana has been through hell," Bet said honestly. "She is only just experiencing freedom for the first time since she was a teenager. She is also newly mated and reunited with her little sister, Jeri. I can't blame her for wanting to stay with her family, now that she finally has one again. Besides, Agnor is a Specitar—a scientist. As are most of the crew of his new ship. It was decided that they would be the best able to deal with whatever we might find here."

"Are you also a scientist?" Lara asked.

"Oh, no. I'm the Loadmaster of the ship. I'm responsible

for the balance, distribution and inventory of the cargo. I'm also..." She blushed, having never admitted this aloud to anyone. "Agnor and I are lovers. It was his Executive Officer who foresaw that both of us should come down to the planet. She has the ability to foresee possibilities for the future."

"Such skills are beyond us," Lara admitted, "but seem wondrous. And you can move things with your mind. I saw what you did. It was very impressive."

Bet was about to reply when she saw Agnor stagger and then move clumsily. A priest ran forward to catch him before he fell, and Bet was on her feet and into the cavern before Lara could say anything. Bet ran over and put her arm around him, supporting him on one side.

"Are you all right?"

"Fine," Agnor said, breathing heavily. "I'll be fine in a minute. It was just a lot to take in. Almost an overload, but I'll be all right. Ki understands our minds better now, I think."

"It is true." The first man who had spoken with them was back, standing in front of Agnor with a phalanx of men behind him.

Bet gasped, worried. Was this going to turn ugly? She sincerely hoped not.

"Ki gives you this gift of itself." The man gestured to the men behind him as he stepped back to allow them to move forward. Each carried a crystal in their hands, each one of different size and shape.

"Ki wishes you to make a study and determine how to make yourselves safe from tyranny. Ki is not a tyrant. Ki does not wish its power to be used to enslave others. Ki craves order, not that individual people be made slaves to it."

Bet didn't really understand, but Agnor nodded, recovering as he took deep breaths. He leaned less on Bet and eventually stood on his own again, the priests facing him, watching him closely.

"Ki does not understand regret, but we do." Lara came forward to speak for the group. "We took the blue man's color as a sign. Looking for portents is, perhaps, a purely human failing. We gave that man the small shards of Ki that occasionally spall off from the main. It was our decision. Our mistake. Our regret."

Agnor kept his silence, and Bet didn't really know what to say. Lara seemed so sad.

"We can fix it," Bet offered. "It won't be easy, but our people have been trying to free those caught by the collective for a long time. They'll find a way."

"I hope you are right," Lara said, then turned toward the path they had taken into the cavern. "I hate to rush you, but over the years, we have become aware how closely our planet is monitored by the blue man's friends. If you are able, sir, you should be on your way as soon as possible. My friends will carry the spallings to your ship and help you settle them. Then they must go back to their areas so the watchers don't get too suspicious."

"I can make it," Agnor said with quiet dignity.

He still seemed pale, as if he'd been through something Bet couldn't quite understand while he'd been communing with Ki. She was curious but counted herself lucky, in a way, that she'd passed out. Agnor looked terrible.

She stuck by his side, allowing him to lean against her shoulder from time to time as they reversed their path back to the ship. The priests were fewer in number, but still with them. And those who carried the so-called spallings were walking with both speed and reverence.

They arrived back at the ship to find it undisturbed. The priests were very efficient in loading the spallings, each of which had a protective pouch made of some natural fiber that was both lightweight and strong. Bet eyed the cargo carefully as it loaded. It would be protected in the fiber cloth, but she quietly directed the priests to place the heavier items in certain locations, careful to balance out the load. Such things would be crucial as they broke through the atmosphere.

Finally, only the main priest and Lara were left. They exchanged formal goodbyes, and Bet thanked the woman for her kindness. The priestly couple retreated, and then finally, Agnor and Bet were free to leave Ipson. Agnor had recovered a bit on the journey back from the cavern, but his color was still a bit pale.

He was able to maneuver the shuttle up through the atmosphere with quiet competence, but he frowned as they started to reach thinner air, miles above the surface. Bet observed him closely, unsure how to help, but ready to step in if he needed her.

"They weren't kidding about being watched," Agnor commented. "We couldn't see them on approach, but from underneath, the sky is filled with satellites. We're lucky we didn't hit anything on the way down." He made a few maneuvers while Bet kept a careful eye on the load of crystals in the back of the small craft. So far, so good. "Hmm. They're going to see that," he muttered. "And…yes. They've detected us. See the attitude of that satellite? It changed to track us. As have the others. Damn."

"What can I do?" Bet asked, trying to be helpful, but feeling quite useless.

"Power down all non-essentials. We don't need comms. I can 'path the ship. In fact, I already have. They're moving into range, matching course and speed. If we can just get there before…"

They both saw it at the same time.

"Oh, shit." It wasn't very ladylike, her aunt would have said, and it was definitely a ground-dweller's term, but it fit the gravity of their new situation.

They watched three enemy ships move out, in formation, from behind a small moon. Other ships did the same from behind another. And then, more made themselves known in other parts of the system. All were broadcasting one message: *Surrender.*

# CHAPTER TWELVE

"No way in hell," Agnor said as he implemented more evasive maneuvers.

Whether the enemy had spotted the *Calypso* or the shuttle, or both, he wasn't sure. Whatever the case, he had no intention of surrendering. Not in this lifetime.

"Divert all power to the shields. We're almost to the *Calypso*."

Bet, bless her heart, was following his commands as if she'd always been on the bridge of a vessel about to come under attack. She was as professional as he could have hoped. She wouldn't fall apart on him. At least, probably not until after they'd escaped. He wouldn't mind it then. About that time, he figured, he'd need a hug too.

An energy weapon clattered against their shields, lighting up the interior of the shuttle with angry red sparks. But the shields held while Agnor 'pathed instructions to Lilith.

A moment later, the *Calypso* was taking the hit, blocking the barrage to the shuttle while Agnor flew it as fast as he dared into the bay.

He'd barely shut down the engines when he felt the *Calypso* sway dangerously.

"That wasn't a beam weapon," Bet whispered, her fingers still flying over the consoles as she helped him shut down the craft.

"Missiles." Agnor unbuckled his safety harness and headed for the exit. "Can you shut down and take care of the cargo?"

Bet looked up and met his gaze for one timeless instant. Emotions passed between them in that moment out of time that they had never spoken aloud. He wanted her to know how he truly felt about her, but there was no time. There would never be time if he didn't get to the bridge and evade the collective's armada.

She nodded, breaking the spell, freeing him to move. Time started up again. He raced out of the shuttle, heading for the bridge at a run.

Bet didn't waste time. She shut down the shuttle so the engines were secure. There were procedures for this, but she had to cut as many corners as she could. They were under attack, and she had to get to the hold and prepare that very special inventory in case the gunners needed replenishment for their ammunition stock.

But she had to take care of the spallings too. Working quickly, she used her telekinetic power to bring a large, empty storage bin from one corner of the bay over to the hatch of the shuttle. One by one, she lifted the wrapped spallings with her mind, placing them gently into the container that had been specially designed for fragile items. It had inflatable walls and dividers which she triggered using her Talent, as each section filled with the precious crystal.

Once they were all transferred and the little ship was secure, Bet wasted no time taking the full container with her out of the bay and into the hold. She stowed it near the door, lashing it down as best she could under the circumstances.

A few of the spallings were very close to the top of the container, but she didn't have time to fix that now. She had felt the shuddering of the ship as it returned fire. The gunners would need to reload soon, and Bet had to be ready to deliver the necessary ammunition.

Using her Talent without hesitation, she maneuvered giant

shipping containers around the hold with precise movements, freeing the ammunition, which had been stored among them, hiding in plain sight. Just as her comm station lit with the automated request for replenishment, Bet was sending the containers down the various corridors, using her Talent to direct them where they were most needed.

Once that was done, she had a moment to spare, to see to the safety of the spallings. As she had feared, one of the medium sized crystals had come out of its protective wrapping. For some odd reason, the crystal itself did not respond to her Talent. She spent a moment puzzling over the fact that she could manipulate the fiber covering, but not the crystal itself, using her telekinesis. Seeing no other alternative, she reached for the crystal, taking it in her bare hand.

And then, everything changed.

Suddenly, she was no longer in the ship. She was no longer really in her body. She could see the placement of all the ships in the enemy armada around her, as if she was the *Calypso*. She could see energy signatures in three-dimensional space without the use of instruments.

It was the crystal. Somehow, it allowed her to see things that she would never have been able to understand before.

She knew what she had to do.

"Sir!" Jemin almost shouted as the enemy ships began moving in impossible ways.

"I see it," Agnor replied. "I see it, but I don't believe it."

He watched, along with the rest of the crew, as each ship in the enemy armada was tossed out of their path, one by one, ship by ship. It looked like nothing Agnor had ever seen before. It almost looked like a child tossing blocks out of its play area, if such a thing were possible with massive ships designed for interstellar travel.

That's about the time Agnor realized he hadn't had the station report from Bet. If she was acting according to protocol, she should have filed the routine report of readiness from her location a few minutes ago. Instead, enemy ships had begun flinging themselves—somehow—far out of the *Calypso's* path.

Agnor began to get an idea of what must be happening. However incredible it seemed, Bet had to be doing something with those ships.

He knew for a fact she was the most powerful telekinetic he had ever known. And if she'd done her job—and he had no reason to doubt her—she now had a load of Ki crystals in the hold with her. It wasn't that far a stretch to think that the two things might be connected.

He worried for her safety. Nobody knew what using the spallings might do to a person. Jana was the only being on a Council world who had ever dealt with the crystal, and she had paid a dear price for it. Agnor wanted to reach out to Bet, but he also didn't want to endanger her by possibly breaking her concentration.

He had to go to her. In person. Now.

Agnor leapt from his command chair and nodded toward Lilith as he headed for the hatch.

"The path is clear. Get us the hell out of here," he ordered, on his way out.

He didn't pause to answer any of the questions he could see in Lilith's eyes. There would be time for that—he hoped—later. Once again, he ran through the ship at full speed, this time heading directly for the cargo hold.

He found Bet there, very close to the hatch, standing stock still, as if she was in a trance. In her hand, one of the spallings glittered, and Bet's lovely dark eyes reflected the blue color of the crystal, the facets sparkling in her gaze.

"Bet? Sweetheart? Are you all right?" Agnor approached slowly.

The spalling she held was one of the larger crystals, about the length of Agnor's hand, tip to tip. It had two points, one on either end, and its clarity was amazing. It glistened and shone in the dark light of the hold, the facets dancing with power.

"Bet?" he asked again, moving closer to her.

She didn't seem able to see him, but her head cocked a bit, toward the sound of his voice.

"Bet? Can you hear me?"

"Agnor?" she whispered in reply.

"I'm here, sweetheart. How are you doing?" He moved cautiously closer.

"It's…it's amazing. Like nothing I've ever experienced before." He heard the true wonder in her voice, but then she frowned. "Are we clear? Why aren't we moving faster?"

"Good question." Agnor wondered why they hadn't taken off as he'd ordered.

He could tell by the pitch of the engines and the vibration of the deck plates that they weren't moving any faster than they had been when he'd made his dash from the bridge. He spared a moment to 'path Lilith.

*"What's happening, Lil? Why are we still here?"* he asked the older woman.

*"It's not for lack of trying,"* Lilith reported back, her tone exasperated. *"We're trying, but something's holding us back."*

"Oh!" Bet exclaimed, drawing Agnor's attention. "I understand now."

"What do you understand, my love?" Agnor asked quietly.

"What Ki wants," she replied in a reasonable tone that Agnor still didn't quite understand. "You'd better tell everybody to brace themselves. Ki is about to clean house, and there are at least three other spallings used by the collective, in the vicinity. We're going to get hit by a power wave, but these crystals in our hold will protect the *Calypso*."

"Oh shit," Agnor whispered, even as he figured out what was about to happen.

He'd lived through the destruction of Jana's control crystal, but if he was interpreting Bet's words correctly, they were about to triple the effect. He ran to the comm and broadcast through the ship.

"Brace, brace, brace!" He shouted. "Incoming power waves. Hold on, people. This is going to be a rough ride."

And then, it hit.

He'd been through something like this before, but not with such intensity. The waves of power shook the ship. Agnor staggered over to Bet and took her in his arms, the crystal be damned.

It glowed with white hot intensity between them, still clutched in her bare hand as he wrapped his arms around her and tried to keep them both on their feet. The crystal's light was almost blinding. He shut his eyes against it, but there was no accompanying heat. The crystal was cool to the touch, but filled with light so bright it hurt to look at it.

The ship shook and wobbled, buffeted by energy waves from the ships that had been tossed out of its path. The collective's armada was still close enough that the destruction of their control crystals affected large swaths of space—including the entire Ipson system.

When the light from the crystal began to die down, Agnor could detect the difference from behind his eyelids. He cracked one, to test whether or not it was safe to open his eyes and found that he could. He looked around the compartment and realized that all the spallings in their fiber coverings were glowing. Their light shone right through the fiber sacks.

*"Lilith? Report if you can,"* Agnor sent telepathically, hoping the crew on the bridge had come through the energy storm intact.

*"We're all right,"* Lilith sent back, though 'pathing wasn't usually her strong suit. *"Everyone's a little stunned, and we're doing assessments now. Looks like..."* She paused for a moment. *"Three of the enemy ships are jettisoning life pods. Each one is near a planet or moon."*

*"Ki is letting the innocent escape before he destroys their ships. Ki doesn't want any more of itself roaming loose among the collective,"* Bet broke in, 'pathing to both Agnor and Lilith as if she'd always done such things. *"Ki will use those shards to seed those worlds with itself. It wants to grow."*

Agnor would consider that startling information later. For now, he had to take stock of the ship, its crew, and what they might be able to do for those refugees from the collective who had just been cut off rather abruptly from its control.

"Honey, can you come with me to the bridge?" Agnor asked Bet, glad to see that her eyes were returning to normal.

No longer did her gaze sparkle with the reflected light of Ki and the stars themselves. Little by little, his Bet, his little mouse, was coming back to him.

"Let me just put this away," she said, moving back and reaching for the fiber cover that had fallen off the spalling in her hand.

With little fuss, she put the crystal away, placing it among the others in the cargo container. She took a moment to stow it all properly, making sure the container's cover was in place so that none of the spallings could break loose again. Then, she turned to him, her eyes bright with accomplishment.

"That was really something, huh?" she said, almost mischievously.

Agnor couldn't help himself. He gathered her in his arms and gave her a swift, deep, exuberant kiss. They didn't have time for more, much to his regret, but he couldn't let the moment pass without demonstrating how much he cared for her.

# CHAPTER THIRTEEN

Hand in hand, they walked onto the bridge a few minutes later. Bet felt the difference immediately. Everyone here had undergone a great shock. Their power was warping and twisting around them in beams of light that, it seemed, only Bet could see.

"Whoa." She stopped short, taking in the scene before her.

"What?" Agnor asked. "What do you see?"

"You probably wouldn't believe it if I could describe it properly. It's like nothing I've ever seen before," she said, staring at the people on the bridge, who were in various stages of recovery. "It's kind of beautiful, actually. The power is dancing around them, resettling into new patterns. Growing. Changing... Becoming."

She stepped onto the bridge, no longer afraid, now that she understood what she was seeing. Her recent experience with Ki had taught her a great deal about how she could visualize the patterns behind each Talent. She had seen it with the ships out there in the Ipson system. She saw it again here, on a smaller scale, but still quite impressive.

"I thought so," Agnor said, pacing beside her. He moved onto the bridge and looked at each member of his crew stationed there, examining them closely.

Bet watched the interplay as Agnor's already formidable energies influenced and touched the newly forming patterns around each person. His care for his people was evident in the way his energies almost cradled theirs, helping where he could, even if he didn't understand the exact mechanism of what he was doing. Bet saw the results as each person gained a bit more control after he talked with them.

Much like the voyage of the *Circe* Bet had read about, where everyone on the crew had gained new levels of power after Jana's control crystal blew up in her hands, something similar had to have happened here. Everyone was dazed, some dealing with it better than others. And everyone looked to Bet like they had new energies wrapping around them.

She had never been able to visualize such things before. Maybe she, too, had gained strength from Ki's influence.

As soon as Agnor seemed satisfied that the bridge crew was all right, he came back to Bet and escorted her to a seat near his command chair. He had to sit at the command station because all the ship's functions he'd need were routed through there, but he looked as if he was loath to let her go. She smiled at him. There would be time for them later. Right now, they had to clean up the situation Ki had made.

She took the secondary comm station and keyed in her identity. She could help by tracking some of the smaller collective ships she had thrown quite far away. Her eyebrows rose as she noted some of the distances. It hadn't felt like much when she was holding that spalling in her hand and hearing the music of the spheres as she walked on the galactic plane. Back here in the real world, what she'd done didn't really seem possible. Not for a normal person.

Then again, Bet had never been normal. She used to resent that fact, but first Agnor, and now Ki, had taught her to revel in it. Nothing wrong with being different. No, not at all.

Agnor was issuing orders to the rest of the crew. She waited for an opening and then sent him the list she had compiled of all the ships she had moved, their current locations, engine status and whatever identifying numbers or names she could glean from her scans.

"Shall I begin contacting them?" she asked when Agnor looked at her with one raised eyebrow. "They're bound to be dazed and probably free of the collective's influence for the first time in years. Some may want to defect."

"Yes," Agnor said quickly. "Yes," he repeated, a bit more calmly. "That's one thing we didn't do at Liata that we should have done right away. Good thinking, Bet. Do it, and offer them conditional asylum if they want to come back to Council space with us."

"Conditional on what?" she challenged, loving the way his gaze glowed with approval. "You know they're going to ask."

Agnor chuckled. "Conditional on a quick examination of each crew member by a Council member. We don't want any of the puppet masters or their sympathizers insinuating themselves onto one of our worlds if we can help it."

Bet nodded, seeing the wisdom in the precaution. "Will do." She turned back to her console and got to work.

What followed was hours of the most exhausting, and rewarding, duty of Bet's life. Every single one of the former collective ships wanted to defect to the Council and agreed to the conditional terms.

Only three of the ships were destroyed as they entered the atmosphere of the planets and moon they orbited. Two of the captains had died as a result of their control crystals shattering, Bet knew. She had been in contact with Ki when it had happened and had felt the crystal entity's acknowledgment of the passing of two sentient beings by its actions.

Those two ships seeded the planets on either side of Ipson. Ki had communicated to Bet that she should make an entry into the stellar databases renaming those planets for the captains who had perished.

Before relinquishing the power Ki had given her—and therefore, direct communication with the entity—she agreed wholeheartedly. When she got back to Geneth Mar, she would make a formal application before the Council, acknowledging Ki's wishes. She would also tell Agnor of the plans Ki had for him, but that could wait.

First, she needed sleep. After the long shift recovering from the energy storm and organizing the retreat from Ipson, she and Agnor retired to his suite together.

He took her in his arms as they lay on his big bed and just held her. She felt safe in a way she never had before. Secure in the knowledge that she loved him and would face whatever happened next full of the power that love gave her. It was stronger than anything in the universe. Even stronger than Ki's influence, or so Ki had claimed when it spoke of Agnor's bond with her.

Ki had seemed to think Agnor loved her too. She hugged that knowledge close, even as she snuggled into Agnor's embrace. Maybe he did. And maybe dreams really did come true.

\* \* \*

It was a ragtag fleet of ships that made their way back to Council space. They had to travel slowly because many of the collective's ships had been damaged in the energy storm. Also, the survivors of the three ships that had been destroyed had to be accommodated on other vessels. There was a bit of overcrowding, but so far, they were all managing.

As they moved slowly through collective space, occasionally, they would be challenged by ships still under the control of the collective. Each time, Bet did her thing, and another ship was added to their little fleet.

After the first battle, she had learned a way to cut the power of the enemy's control crystals without having to blow them up. Ki, through the spallings and Bet's mind, was somehow able to recall—or maybe *reprogram* would be a better word—the crystals on the enemy ships, blocking their control over the crew and captains.

Once that link was severed, the captains were usually glad to hand over the instruments that had kept them enslaved.

Bet was amassing quite a collection of control scepters, shards and spallings. She had been able to fill another of the small storage containers in the hold so far, and they were only about halfway home.

Soon though, they would be in Council space. Unless the collective wanted to invade, Bet thought they would most likely cut their losses and let the small fleet of defectors go. At least, she hoped for that outcome. She didn't want to have to cause anyone harm. The *Calypso* was very low on ammunition, so any defense would most likely be up to Bet. She would do what she had to do when called upon, but she didn't really enjoy violence. It went against her nature.

She would do all she could to protect her people, but she couldn't help feeling sorry for those who tried to stand in their way. Agnor tried to help her focus on the many Talents they had freed from the collective on this journey. That helped. Each ship held souls that would be free to choose their own path now. There was a beautiful sort of justice in that.

Bet didn't see a lot of Agnor in the days following. They were both kept busy with the occasional confrontations and then the aftermath of each new ship joining their little fleet. Bet was in charge of all the spallings and collected control devices of surrendered ships. She was run ragged obtaining them and then securing them in the hold, while Agnor did his job on the bridge.

They slept together every time they were off shift, but new challenges arrived almost constantly in the first few days of their journey. After the initial surge to try to stop the *Calypso*, the enemy attacks came less frequently, but they still came at all hours. More than once, Bet and Agnor had been dragged out of sleep by the need to respond to some new threat.

Eventually, though, they crossed into Council space and, as she'd hoped, the collective's attacks dropped to nothing. The little fleet of ships limped along, heading for Geneth Mar on the closest possible route.

"We're not quite home free yet," Agnor had told her as

they snuggled in his bed during the first off-shift they'd spent where nothing had disturbed them. They'd both have to be back on duty soon, but they had a few minutes to laze together and cuddle.

"But we're less likely to encounter problems now that we're in Council space, right?" she asked, tracing patterns on his chest with a lazy fingertip.

"Yeah, and although we didn't mean to, we've been decimating the collective's fleet. We never had a completely accurate count of how many warships they had, but even so, the sheer number of ships that we've liberated has to hurt. I wonder if Ki knew this was going to happen?"

"I think Ki probably suspected as much when it gave me the power to retune the collective's control crystals. I got the distinct feeling that Ki would be glad to break the enslavement of whatever minds we happened to crossed paths with along our journey." Bet sat up, knowing they needed to start getting ready for the day ahead. "Ki isn't exactly benevolent, but it does not enjoy loss of life."

"In my talks with Ki, I got a sense that it was unlike any other life form we've ever encountered in its way of thinking. It has its own code of behavior, and its own expectations of others," Agnor said as he rose from the bed and stretched. "I was very concerned, at first, that it wanted to expand to those other planets and that moon, but I've come to realize that Ki has a right to live and grow, as do we all."

"It doesn't like its spallings being used to subjugate other minds. Ki helps bring order, where wanted. It doesn't seek to impose it against another being's free will."

She stepped into the sonic shower to quickly clean up, unsurprised when Agnor followed her. After a quick blast of cleaning pulses, he shut off the unit and crowded her against one smooth wall, bracketing her between his outstretched arms.

"Speaking of free will…"

Agnor hesitated, which was very unlike him. Bet reached out and cupped his cheek in one palm. She saw the struggle in his gaze. The uncertainty.

She took a chance and made the leap he seemed afraid to broach.

"I love you, Agnor."

Bet didn't dare breathe, waiting for his reply. Had she just screwed everything up? Had she misread him? She wanted to cringe, but maybe…just maybe…

# CHAPTER FOURTEEN

Agnor let go of the breath he'd unconsciously been holding.

"Oh, thank the stars. I love you too, Bet. With all my heart."

He dipped his head to capture her lips. He couldn't wait to show her how he felt. They didn't have a lot of time, but that never stopped them. Bet was his match in every way.

He felt her warm skin against his, and all the feelings he'd hidden away deep inside came out in a rush. He wanted forever with Bet. Forever. With her alone. It was an astounding thought to a man who had been with so very many women in his years, but somehow, all those experiences had been preparing him for this. For perfection. With Bet.

Tears formed behind his eyes as he held her. They'd been through so much in the past days. The danger of confronting the priests and then the danger inherent in making first contact with a new and unusual life form. Those long minutes when Bet had been unconscious had nearly killed him with worry.

He'd realized then that, if she had died, he would have tried to follow. He wouldn't have wanted to live without her. After experiencing the glory of her love, he couldn't go back to the superficial joinings of his past. He had witnessed the true bonds between Micah and Jeri, Darak and Jana. He had wanted that, and he had found it. With Bet.

He kissed her deeply, pouring all the love into his touch that he possibly could, hoping she understood how precious she was to him. He would show her again and again, every day of their lives, if only she would consent to be his.

*"I love you, Bet. I've never said that to anyone else. I've never felt like this about anyone else. You're it for me,"* he said within the intimacy of their shared minds, laying his soul bare to her.

He practically held his breath as he awaited her answer. He lifted his mouth from hers and kissed his way down her neck, pressing close against her.

*"I feel the same,"* she replied finally, seeming to hesitate just the tiniest bit. He didn't like that.

Agnor drew back a few inches to meet her gaze. He paused to emphasize the seriousness of the moment.

"I want to spend the rest of my life with you, Bet. I want you to be my life partner. My mate. My lover. My wife." His voice gentled as he saw the tears in her eyes.

"I want that too. But are you really sure? Agnor, you could have your choice of any woman you wanted."

Agnor didn't like the uncertainty in her words, but he would show her—for the rest of their lives—how wrong she was to doubt him. He would make it his life's work to prove his love to her, each and every day.

"You are all I have ever wanted. You are the woman I have been searching for, unconsciously, my whole life. I have never been more certain of anything as I am of my love for you. I need you by my side, facing life's challenges, Bet. You. And only you. For as long as we live."

Finally, an incandescent happiness seemed to replace doubt in her gaze, and he stepped closer, sealing his declaration with a deep and fiery kiss. He cupped her breasts, massaging the tender tips, enjoying the feel of her response to his touch. She writhed against him as her passion mounted, making those soft little sounds that drove him wild.

Unable to hold back, any longer, he lifted her legs, and she eagerly wrapped them around his waist. She was slick and hot against his cock, both of them ready for anything after all they'd been through. Still, he paused long enough to check on her. Her comfort would always come first with him.

*"Do you want me now, my love?"* he 'pathed to her receptive mind.

*"Come into me, Agnor. Please. Don't make me wait. I need you."*

"That's just what I wanted to hear," he all but growled, speaking aloud in his haste to be inside her.

He held her gaze as he pushed inside, slow and steady, until he was deep within her, and they were one. He did something then that he had never done with any other lover—he deliberately meshed their minds, dropping his guard to her and her alone, letting Bet inside the shields he kept rigorously tight against all others. Only for her, would he ever drop his shields.

He felt the touch of Bet's mind as he began moving within her. He hoped she knew how much he loved the feel of her accepting him, welcoming him, taking him in and giving her all in return. It was a profound moment, full of promise and potential. His lips sought hers as he repeatedly thrust into her slick heat, pumping them both toward an ecstasy he'd only ever found in her arms.

*"Do you understand what you are to me?"* he asked in the privacy of their joined minds. Emotion engulfed his thoughts—his, hers, theirs.

He didn't know exactly where he ended and she began, and it was the most fulfilling thing he had ever experienced. Even as their bodies strained toward completion, their minds interwove and formed a new, thrilling creation that was...more. Bigger, stronger, more powerful, but also more emotion-filled, more loving and caring. More...everything.

If Agnor had harbored any doubts, he now knew they were meant to be this. They were better together than they ever would be apart. They needed each other to complete each of their souls, and he never wanted to be apart from her ever again. He just had to make her understand his need was more than for just this moment out of time. He had to make sure she wanted this communion of the spirit for keeps—or at least as often as they could manage this sort of joining over the next hundred years or so.

*"I am…everything?"* she answered, her thoughts powerful in their confusion as the sensations he was creating within her body threatened to overcome her rational mind.

*Not yet,* he hoped silently. They were on the brink of something here even more momentous than the physical pleasure they created together.

*"Yes, my Bet. You are everything to me. All that I am. All that I may yet become. All that we can be together. Do you understand?"*

He wanted so desperately for her to give it all to him. Her body, her mind, and now her soul. But she was too far gone. The pleasure beckoned and he was as powerless as she was to deny the explosion of their shared climax. His body spasmed in ecstasy as she cried out his name, over and over.

Physical pleasure overcame them, even as the emotional component added something never before experienced to the climax. Agnor gasped, his breath short as his body tried to deal with the firestorm of pleasure on every level. He felt Bet tremble in his arms as she dealt with the same. Their minds blasted apart at the last, unwinding in a gentle slide that only added to the sensation of being caressed on every level.

It was like nothing he could ever have imagined. It was the most complete immersion in orgasm on every level—physical, mental and even spiritual—that he had ever experienced. And he wanted more. So much more. He wanted that every time. Every day. It was like a new drug that, once tasted, was always craved. And the drug was love in its purest, rarest form.

Distilled perfection.

Agnor held Bet as she gasped along with him. Gradually, their breathing quieted, as they came back to themselves.

"You are amazing, Bet," Agnor praised her when he could speak again.

She snuggled against his chest, her head resting on his

shoulder. "You too, Ag."

She sounded adorably worn out. He roused her briefly to cycle through the cleaning pulses again, amused by the way she let him take charge.

She seemed to revive as soon as they were both clean again, and his thoughts turned to the big bed waiting for them in his quarters. But, no. He had to resist the temptation to find that nirvana of pleasure again.

He wished he could just take this shift off and spend it in bed with her, but duty called, and he was the captain. There were things only he could deal with. Just as there were responsibilities in the cargo hold that only Bet could see to. Most especially the very rare collection of spallings, control scepters and other bits of Ki that only Bet seemed both capable and willing to deal with.

Reality came back to him with a crash. They both had responsibilities, much as he'd rather just make the world go away and spend time with her. He carried her into his chamber and placed her on the bed—seating her on the side of it, not lying in the center, spread eagled, the way he really wanted her. He was trying hard to be good. The ship needed them both, he reminded himself. There would be time for more divine sex later.

But before they each left for their duty stations, Agnor had one thing he wanted to make perfectly clear. They dressed quietly, each a little wrung out from the emotional storm of their lovemaking, the admissions of love and the aftermath. By the time Agnor was fully dressed, he'd regained a bit of his equilibrium. He took Bet by the hand and urged her to sit beside him on the edge of the bed.

"I meant every word of what I said before," he began, wanting to solidify the promises they had made in passion, now, when they were both calmer and thinking more clearly. "I love you."

"Me too," she replied in a quiet tone he noticed she used when she was feeling uncertain.

It enchanted him that she could still feel shy around him.

Perhaps she would never outgrow that habitual timidity—and he found he didn't mind that at all. She was who she was, and he loved every facet of her being.

"That being the case..." Agnor slid off the edge of the bed to kneel at her feet. "Would you do me the great honor of marrying me?"

Her little sob of joy rang through his heart as a few precious tears flowed down her face.

"Yes," she choked out. "Oh, yes."

She reached for him, and he reclaimed his seat on the bed, next to her, taking her into his arms and squeezing her tight while she clung to him. He stroked her hair, happiness filling him.

"I want the whole galaxy to know how much I love you, Bet. I want us to be partners in life and love for the rest of our days," he declared softly, loving the feel of her in his arms. Loving her.

"I want that too," she finally managed to say as her tears subsided. "I love you so much."

And then, she reached up and kissed him, putting all the love in her heart into the kiss that stole his breath.

\* \* \*

Agnor was in regular contact with some of the stronger telepathic minds on Geneth Mar. His telepathy had taken another giant leap in strength when the energy waves had hit them above Ipson. Everyone on the ship had gained power from the experience, much like what had happened on the *Circe* during the battle with Jana's armada.

Since then, however, with Ki's influence and Bet's ability to direct the power of the spallings, they'd avoided any more uncontrolled explosions. Everybody had been spared further upset.

The new ability to contact multiple minds on Geneth Mar, and many more on the planets they passed closer to, helped tremendously in the planning and disposition of the enemy fleet. Rather than escort a flotilla of former enemy ships deep into the heart of Council space, they were able to divide the ships into much smaller groups, dropping them at various points along their course for examination.

Specialists had been dispatched from Geneth Mar and also taken from among the populations of the planets they passed, to interview the crews and grant them asylum or passage to wherever they wished to go. Many of the non-Talented foot soldiers, for example, wanted to return to their planets of origin. The Council was already making plans to help those people repatriate, though it would take some time to get them back home. In the meantime, small groups were cautiously given quarters on various Council worlds and were monitored closely, though not imprisoned.

The Talents pretty much uniformly applied for political asylum. They didn't want to go anywhere near the collective. Not for a good long while.

Most of those poor souls had lost years of their lives, unable to remember what they had done or where they had been. Some had been taken as children by the collective and were now close to retirement age, with no recollection of what had come in between.

Counselors were found for those sad cases, and all freed Talents were given at least some therapy to help them deal with what had been done to them. Each Talented mind was examined in the process and a few were found that had actually volunteered for the collective. Some were power hungry, and remained so.

Some had actively participated in atrocities. Those few were arrested and detained while cases were built against them. Trials would commence as soon as possible.

Agnor supervised all as they made their way slowly home. He also quietly retested each member of his crew, assigning new designations for them all and committing those who were having trouble with their new abilities to extra training.

By the time they arrived back home, they had only a few of the surrendered ships with them, and the process had been streamlined. Agnor and his crew were able to leave that work to others while they made their report directly to the Council.

Bet was in sole charge of the very precious cargo they were to deliver, and she wouldn't allow any of the usual cargo handling equipment near the two containers. Instead, she moved them using her Talent alone. Agnor had discussed it with her beforehand. In addition to being safer for such delicate treasures, now that Bet's ability was off the charts as far as strength and reliability went, it would also speak very eloquently about her standing.

Bet may have left Geneth Mar inconspicuously, but she was going to arrive back home in style. Agnor was going to see to it. All those people who had underestimated or overlooked her all these years were about to get a very rude awakening.

He even had some covert plans for Bet's reunion with her aunt. She'd told him more about her home life and upbringing over the past days, and Agnor knew there were unresolved emotional issues surrounding Bet's Aunt Petra and the way Bet had been raised. Agnor couldn't wait to see how the older woman responded to this new, confident and strong Bet. He planned to have a front row seat to see how it all played out—and to be there to support Bet, should she need him.

He thought maybe, at this point, she was plenty strong enough to handle anything her aunt could dish out, but he'd be there, just to make sure. He knew it was important for her to come to terms with her past so they could move forward into the future…together.

Her Talents had increased so much over the past weeks. Her new power was almost incalculable. Like his own. They'd changed on a fundamental level with all that had happened, and the steady diet of energizing, fulfilling-on-every-level sex had only added to their abilities.

There was no down time anymore. If one or the other of them were feeling fatigued from using their vastly expanded Talents, a sharing of love would set them right in no time flat.

In fact, it made them even stronger.

Which only went to prove a hypothesis Agnor had held for a long time... Love truly was the strongest power in the universe.

Bet's ability to read minds would remain a closely guarded secret for now. Even if the collective was no longer the force it had once been, her Talent might yet come in handy. Agnor and Bet would tell only the highest levels of their government about her mind-reading skills. In the meantime, her telekinetic abilities were enough to wow anyone. He couldn't wait to see the reaction to her no-longer-hidden Talent.

When they docked at the orbital station, much to Agnor's surprise, Micah, Jeri, Jana and Darak were there, waiting for them. Agnor was hugged and clapped on the back by all four. When he introduced Bet as his fiancée, he received another round of hugs and congratulations, as did Bet.

The foursome had arranged a private room for a quick debrief before Agnor and his crew went before the Council. Since Micah and Jeri were two of the most powerful Talents in the galaxy, they got pretty much anything they asked for. In this case, a few hours with Agnor before he had to report to the Council seemed a small enough concession.

Bet was shy with his friends at first, but Agnor kept her near as they sat in a comfortable lounge. Each couple had been given a plush couch placed around a low, central table that had been laden with all sorts of finger foods. Agnor snagged a plate and loaded it with things he thought Bet would like, sharing the plate with her as they sat side by side. The others were relaxed, which helped Bet relax too. Once they'd caught up on personal stuff and eaten a bit, Micah got down to business.

"What everyone wants to know is, how in the world did you manage to capture so many enemy ships?" Micah asked bluntly.

Agnor had 'pathed some of this already to Micah and several other strong minds, but he had known the real explanation couldn't be made until they were face to face. He motioned to Bet, and she took the wrapped spalling he'd asked her to carry out of her bag. Gently, she removed the fiber covering, though she didn't touch the crystal itself with her bare hands. They both knew by now that, if she touched the crystal directly, her consciousness would be transported to that galactic plane on which she'd operated to disable all those ships.

"When we got to Ipson, this is what we found," Agnor said quietly while everyone seemed mesmerized by the sparkle of the large, double-terminated crystal. "It is a small part of Ki. What it calls a spalling. Ki gifted this to us, along with others like it in different sizes, once we had proved ourselves to it."

"How did you manage that?" Jeri whispered, still staring at the crystal.

"Bet made first contact simply by lowering her shields. Nobody knew this before we started our journey, and I don't intend for any but the highest in our government to know now, but Bet has a very powerful and accurate mind-reading Talent. She was able to read, and be read by, Ki. That paved our way."

Darak's shrewd eyes shifted from the glittering crystal to Bet. Darak looked her over, as if appraising her, and Agnor bristled a bit. Darak may be happily mated now to Jana, but he had always been a rogue and inveterate ladies man.

"You are a lady of hidden Talents," Darak said, tipping his imaginary hat to her as Bet blushed.

"Once Ki had accepted us, I was allowed to make direct contact via telepathy. I don't know how long it took..." Agnor trailed off, still not sure how long he had stood there in the crystal cavern, communing with Ki.

"It was over an hour," Bet supplied quietly. "Closer to two or three, maybe. I lost track of time too, but Lara, the priestess, came to get me eventually. I sat with her for a while, watching you from the antechamber."

Agnor covered her free hand with his, squeezing lightly. *"I didn't know that,"* he 'pathed privately to her. *"Thank you for watching over me, my love."*

"Priestess?" Jana asked, unknowingly interrupting their private moment. "There are people on Ipson that serve this…Ki?" She looked upset by the idea, but Bet was quick to set her straight.

"The people on Ipson have no Talent. That's the way Ki wants it. Ki promotes order in all things and helps others find it, if they wish it, but Ki has no desire to enslave Talented minds," Bet told them. "It was Ki that disabled the collective's control crystals, working through the spallings and through me." Bet blushed a bit more. "That's what allowed me to retune the crystals in the enemy ships and free the trapped minds. Ki wanted them free. Ki never intended for its order to be imposed unwillingly on any human mind."

"And Ki is expanding," Agnor put in, knowing they had to hear this. "The system containing Ipson has two other planets and a moon that are now seeded with old, shattered control crystals. Two collective captains died in the process. This was before Ki and Bet had worked out how to do the retuning without overloading the crystals to the point where they exploded."

Jana looked shaken. "I'm glad you figured that one out." Her own permanently attached crystals sparkled in the light of the room.

"Ki felt bad about the death of those two captains. Ki wishes to name the two planets after them, in their memory."

"This Ki is sentient? It has feelings?" Micah asked shrewdly.

"It's not exactly the way we comprehend emotion," Agnor explained. "Ki is timeless. It doesn't age, though it does understand time's passage as it relates to its surroundings and the priests that live on Ipson. I think it started communicating with the people on Ipson as a way to learn about our species, even though it's hard for Ki to commune with an un-Talented mind."

"Ki implied that it had learned the danger it posed to Talents at some time in the past. It sensed its order could be imposed on weaker minds, and luckily, it believes that is a bad thing. Order is what Ki is all about. It likes to encourage it in other beings, but only if it is welcome. Ki seems to understand that not all beings are—or even want to be—as well-ordered as it is."

"Crystals grow in certain, rigid structures," Agnor told them. "Ki is essentially a crystal that can only grow in certain paths and directions, according to the physical laws of the universe. It likes order because it cannot grow or be any other way. That structure is also incredibly powerful and is a fantastic conduit for psi energy, which is where the conflict comes in. Ki is aware of the danger and was very careful to examine our character and all of my memories before it allowed us to be its champion. It gave us only a small sample of itself for study and reference, but it also gave it as a way to communicate directly with Ki."

Bet lifted the spalling to show them again. "Through this, some of us can commune with Ki, and it can check up on us, as well. That was the condition of our alliance. Ki gave us the power—and the duty—to relieve the collective of as many of the spallings and shards the puppet masters had taken over the years and used so evilly. In return, we have promised never to use Ki's order for evil, to keep Talented minds away from the Ipson system, and to communicate with Ki via the spallings so that we may continue to exchange learning and information."

"You made an alliance with it?" Darak asked.

Agnor smiled. "You bet we did. Ki considered the previous alliance it had with the collective, through the puppet master named Kol, to be null and void. Kol lied, and if he weren't already dead, Ki would have demanded he be brought to trial. Ki is allied with the Council now, under much stricter conditions than it had with the collective. It has learned from its mistakes. There will be checks and balances this time. But since Ki is expanding, it realized it needed allies to help keep unscrupulous Talents from its system. That's where the Council comes in."

"It sounds like this is the end of the collective," Jeri said, her voice tinged with hope.

# CHAPTER FIFTEEN

"In essence, it is," Bet pronounced, the room stilling for a breathless moment before she continued. "It will take some time for us to ferret out all the remaining spallings and shards, but we have the power to nullify them now."

"Ki has asked that we eventually return those pieces to the Ipson system to seed the other moons. It will take time, but Ki wants to expand to take over the entire system," Agnor told them, sitting forward to make a map of sorts out of olives and rolls. "These are the planets in the system. This one…" he stuck a cocktail fork in the top of one of the rolls he'd laid out, "…is Ipson. These are the two that have already been seeded." He added two more forks in two more of the rolls. "These are the moons." He pointed to several olives he'd laid out around the rolls. "This one was just seeded." He bit that olive in half and put one half back down on the table, eating the other half. "The rest are ripe for the crystals we have retrieved from the collective. Ki wants us to return in one standard year and do it."

"What about expansion beyond the Ipson system?" Micah asked, studying the crude diagram on the table.

"For now, Ki has no interest in that. Its experiences with humans so far has led it to believe that it should centralize its location," Bet said quietly.

"The potential for misuse is greater if Ki is spread out all over the galaxy. If it is limited to one system, it's easier to protect," Agnor added. "Plus, you have to understand the timelines we're talking about. Ki doesn't grow overnight. The structure of Ki on Ipson took millennia to develop. Seeding the system is just the first step in a very long process by human standards. Ki probably won't want to expand again—if it ever does—for several thousand years. Maybe longer."

"Time just isn't the same for Ki as it is for us," Bet reflected. She offered the crystal up for examination again. "I know you won't want to take the chance now, but after the Specitars have finished examining the spallings, you should commune with Ki. You'd understand it all a lot better."

"What do you see when you use the crystal?" Jana wanted to know.

"It takes me out of this plane of existence, onto a sort of galactic plane. I can see the *Calypso* as if I'm standing on top of it, and I can see all the enemy ships. And I can use my telekinesis, augmented by Ki, into something that allows me to move entire ships full of people across solar systems."

"It's pretty astounding to watch the results when Bet gets into battle mode," Agnor said, running his hand down her back, stroking her.

He was so damned proud of her. She'd blossomed into the most amazing woman, though she retained that indefinable something that made her Bet. He loved every inch of her. Every gesture. Every smile.

"That sounds amazing," Jana said, smiling now.

She was a tough woman to get to know, but she seemed more at ease now than Agnor had ever seen her. Darak was good for her. Their mating was a solid one that had brought them both a measure of peace. Agnor thought he understood it now. Now that he had Bet in his life.

"What you're describing sounds familiar," Jana went on, talking to Bet. "Memories of some of the things I did while under control of the collective are still coming back to me. When I got the name StarKiller, it was because I somehow managed to stop a star from destroying the planet Plectar. I remember looking down on the system in the way you just described, like I was outside my ship, walking among the planets and stars. I thought I was dreaming, but after hearing what you've just said, I think it was Ki helping save all those lives on Plectar. Ki working through me, somehow."

"It's very possible," Bet said, encouragement ringing in her tone. "Ki respects life. It would act to save it, if it were possible."

Jana and Bet kept talking about different aspects of their experiences with Ki while Micah leaned over to speak to Agnor.

"Your lady is really something, Ag," Micah said with a smile. "I'm very happy for you."

"Thanks," Agnor replied, watching Bet talk with Jana, her face animated with excitement as her shyness retreated in the face of acceptance. His friends had accepted her, and Agnor felt a warm glow in his heart for them and for her. There was nothing better in this life than the love of friends and especially the love of a true soul mate.

"Have you given any thought to how the Council is going to react?" Micah broke in on Agnor's happy thoughts.

"React to what? The crystals? I figured they'd cause quite a stir."

"The crystals, yes..." Micah trailed off, which drew Agnor's full attention. "But what I was really thinking of was you and your lady. You missed some things while you were on your mission to Ipson. Darak and Jana have been retested and both are now Shas, just like Jeri and me. I think I'm looking at two more in you and Bet, if I'm not very much mistaken."

Agnor was floored. Sha was the highest rank a Talant could attain. There were only ever a handful of Shas in each generation. Sometimes, only one or two. If Micah was right—and Agnor had no reason to doubt his old friend—this little lounge held six of the most powerful Talents in the galaxy.

And he was one of them. And Bet too.

Well...of course they were Shas. Who better? And who else could have taken down the collective with only two lives lost and thousands freed?

"We did experience another energy storm when those three crystals shattered above Ipson," Agnor thought aloud. "I knew the whole crew gained a level or two, but there was nobody available to test me, and I'm not very objective when it comes to Bet, so I left her retesting until we got home."

"We'll make it all official later, but there's little doubt in my mind right now, Ag. Welcome to the highest rank there is." Micah reached over and shook Ag's hand, wearing a big grin. "Life is about to get really strange."

Micah hadn't been kidding. In the weeks that followed, Agnor and Bet did, indeed, test out as Shas. They were given all sorts of acclaim for having returned to Geneth Mar triumphant and routing the collective.

There was still much to do. Jana and Darak took up the cause of the collective's conscripted army. They were organizing the ranks and helping repatriate those soldiers who wanted to go back to their homeworlds. Micah and Jeri handled the political aspects of being Shas. They interfaced with the Council more than any of the other newly minted Shas, and Agnor was just as happy to leave them to it. Politics wasn't his thing.

Instead, he and Bet had been working on the scientific side of things. They were overseeing all work with the crystals, and Bet was in charge of their storage and care. The spallings Ki had given them were alive in a way the crystals the collective had been given weren't. Because of that, they needed extra care, and because of the added dimension of conscious life, they were able to allow communication back to their source.

It was a time of discovery and innovation. Communication and the building of relationships between two very different species.

Agnor also loved working with Bet every day. He loved the fact that she was now treated with the respect she should always have gotten and that she was coming out of her shell more and more, but still retained that quiet, gentle way that made her so very appealing. He just loved her. Period.

They had made plans for their wedding. It was supposed to be a small affair, but for the two newest Shas on Geneth Mar, a small wedding was just not possible. Jeri and Jana had turned their little ceremony into something for the ages, but Agnor didn't mind, as long as Bet was happy.

Finally, the day arrived, and Agnor met her in front of the crowd of well-wishers and friends. They exchanged their vows and pledged their troth. They had a big party, surrounded by those who had come to celebrate their union. The day, and the night, that followed were absolutely perfect.

"I love you, my husband." Bet reached upward to kiss him.

"I love you, my wife," he replied, kissing her back.

Bet sighed happily and laid her head against his shoulder. "I don't think I'll ever get tired of hearing that."

"Me neither," he agreed, feeling smugly happy, alone at last with his new spouse.

"I can't believe the collective has just about collapsed," she said quietly, running her fingers along his arm idly.

"There are a few pockets, but we can take the *Calypso* out again in a few weeks and free those poor souls who are still trapped." Personally, he wouldn't rest until every captured Talent was freed.

"I'd like that. Nobody should be controlled like that."

Agnor knew she'd seen a lot as she had freed so many of the collective's victims. So had he.

"We won't stop, my love. Not until every last one of them is free."

With that vow ringing through his mind, Agnor finally slept, secure in the arms of his soul mate.

# # #

# ABOUT THE AUTHOR

Bianca D'Arc has run a laboratory, climbed the corporate ladder in the shark-infested streets of lower Manhattan, studied and taught martial arts, and earned the right to put a whole bunch of letters after her name, but she's always enjoyed writing more than any of her other pursuits. She grew up and still lives on Long Island, where she keeps busy with an extensive garden, several aquariums full of very demanding fish, and writing her favorite genres of paranormal, fantasy and sci-fi romance.

Bianca loves to hear from readers and can be reached through Twitter (@BiancaDArc), Facebook (BiancaDArcAuthor) or through the various links on her website.

### WELCOME TO THE D'ARC SIDE...
### WWW.BIANCADARC.COM

# OTHER BOOKS BY BIANCA D'ARC

*Brotherhood of Blood*
One & Only
Rare Vintage
Phantom Desires
Sweeter Than Wine
Forever Valentine
Wolf Hills
Wolf Quest

*Tales of the Were*
Lords of the Were
Inferno

*Tales of the Were – The Others*
Rocky
Slade

*Tales of the Were – Redstone Clan*
The Purrfect Stranger
Grif
Red
Magnus
Bobcat
Matt

*String of Fate*
Cat's Cradle
King's Throne
Jacob's Ladder
Her Warriors

*Grizzly Cove*
All About the Bear
Mating Dance
Night Shift
Alpha Bear

*Dragon Knights*
Maiden Flight
The Dragon Healer
Border Lair
Master at Arms
The Ice Dragon
Prince of Spies
Wings of Change
FireDrake
Dragon Storm
Keeper of the Flame
Hidden Dragons

*Resonance Mates*
Hara's Legacy
Davin's Quest
Jaci's Experiment
Grady's Awakening
Harry's Sacrifice

*Jit'Suku Chronicles*
*Arcana:* King of Swords
*Arcana:* King of Cups
*Arcana:* King of Clubs
*Arcana:* King of Stars
End of the Line

*StarLords*
Hidden Talent
Talent For Trouble
Shy Talent

*Gifts of the Ancients*
Warrior's Heart

*Guardians of the Dark*
Half Past Dead
Once Bitten, Twice Dead
A Darker Shade of Dead
The Beast Within
Dead Alert

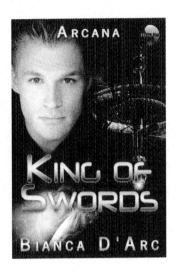

## *ARCANA*
## KING OF SWORDS

David is a newly retired special ops soldier, looking to find his way in an unfamiliar civilian world. His first step is to visit an old friend, the owner of a bar called *The Rabbit Hole* on a distant space station. While there, he meets an intriguing woman who holds the keys to his future.

Adele has a special ability, handed down through her family. Adele can sometimes see the future. She doesn't know exactly why she's been drawn to the space station where her aunt deals cards in a bar that caters to station workers and ex-military. She only knows that she needs to be there. When she meets David, sparks of desire fly between them and she begins to suspect that he is part of the reason she traveled halfway across the galaxy.

Pirates gas the inhabitants of the station while Adele and David are safe inside a transport tube and it's up to them to repel the invaders. Passion flares while they wait for the right moment to overcome the alien threat and retake the station. But what good can one retired soldier and a civilian do against a ship full of alien pirates?

# EXCERPT

**King of Swords** by Bianca D'Arc

*Jit'Suku Chronicles ~ Arcana #1*

Adele pushed through the portal and waited a moment for her eyes to adjust to the gloom inside. What she could see of the place was clean and well kept. The atmosphere was dark, quiet and relaxing rather than sinister as she'd half expected. She noted the big men at the bar as her eyes adjusted slowly, scanning the room for her aunt. The place was set up with small private booths and one long bar area where the men clustered. Soldiers, they had to be, though they were all in civ clothing. On leave or perhaps retirees, she guessed, noting the bartender looked to built on the same grand scale. Soldiers were just bigger than regular human males. It had something to do with their diet and training, she knew, but other than that, she hadn't paid much attention.

Unlike many civilians, Adele had no real opinion about soldiers. Oh, she appreciated the sacrifices they made trying to keep the Milky Way Galaxy safe from the jit'suku threat, but she'd never really had any dealings with them on a personal basis. She knew many civ men discriminated against them-probably because they felt small by comparison.

She'd seen soldiers here and there throughout her travels and to a man they were all huge and rather intimidating. She supposed a civilian man would feel a little threatened by their towering height and imposing brawn, but she felt somehow comforted by their large, protective presence. Surely, if men such as these were fighting the jit'suku out on the rim, the rest of humanity would always be safe. They inspired that kind of confidence with their silent, somewhat menacing ways.

Adele swept the room once again but didn't see her aunt, so she decided to brave the quiet crowd at the bar to ask. She walked to an open space, feeling enclosed by the heat of the big men sitting on either side of her, but she refused to acknowledge the sort of tingly reaction that skittered through her body. It wasn't fear exactly, but it was definitely something that surprised her.

"Pardon me," she said in a voice that carried to the bartender. All eyes turned to her and she found herself the unexpected center of attention. "Can you tell me if Della Senna is here? I understand she's dealing here now." The bartender slung a towel over his shoulder and walked toward her with a rolling gait that oozed sex appeal. She'd never been this close to a soldier, much less half a dozen of them, and each and every one was solidly built, and handsome as sin. This bartender was perhaps the prettiest of the bunch, with perfectly chiseled features and a confident, friendly expression.

When he smiled, she felt the bottom fall out of her stomach. He was definitely what her old friend Mary would label DDG—Drop Dead Gorgeous.

"Della's on break, but she'll be back in about five minutes if you want to wait."

His deep voice sent little shivers down her spine. The man was sexy as hell and dangerous to boot. She could feel it crackling in the air around him as he stopped right in front of her on the other side of the bar. She was glad of the hard metal of the bar between them. His attention shifted to the man seated on her right. A slight nod and narrowing of his eyes was all that was needed to make the other man jump into action. A moment later, he'd drawn a barstool up behind her and politely assisted her to sit.

"Thank you." She looked over at the man on the right, surprised by his youth. This soldier was definitely younger than her and his clothes looked brand new. Perhaps he was on leave. She smiled at him and his face seemed to heat just the tiniest bit with a flush of embarrassment. She liked the young man immediately. He was polite and a little shy, which surprised her even more. Built like a freighter, she wouldn't have imagined anything as simple as a smile could fluster him, but apparently it did.

"What'll you have, ma'am?" The bartender polished a

small glass and set it before her, probably assuming she'd have a typical girly drink suited to the petite glass. Feeling daring, she smiled with an air of challenge. "Do you have any Pearson's Star Ale on tap?"

The bartender straightened and smiled, taking the little glass away. "Indeed I do. Coming right up."

When he turned to fetch her ale, she was treated to a lovely view of his sculpted ass. The man was pure muscle and his formfitting pants showed his assets off to best advantage. She'd bet he made great tips from the ladies based just on his butt alone. Sighing, she and sat back on the surprisingly comfortable stool. She didn't feel as out of place here as she'd feared. The atmosphere was quiet, but welcoming.

A moment later the handsome bartender was back, placing a frothy, frosted pint before her with relish. Adele licked her lips, staring at the perfectly poured portion. She had a taste for this particular brew and didn't partake of it often due to its hefty price, but this occasion seemed to call for it. With relish, she took a sip of the thick, dark ale and the taste exploded on her tongue.

"Mmm, delicious."

She moved to get her credit chit, but a big hand swooped in from the side, pressing a credit chit into the bartender's hand.

"Allow me, ma'am."

Startled, she looked over to acknowledge the huge man sitting to her left. Blonde and blue eyed, this guy was a little older than her. Probably a retiree, and a recent one, if the newness of his clothing was anything to go by. Soldiers didn't usually have a lot of money to spare when they left the service and this ale was a luxury. She couldn't let him pay for it in good conscience, though it was a lovely gesture.

"That's very kind of you but-"

"It would be my pleasure. My name is David." His smile totally disarmed her. It was even more devastating than the bartender's.

"I'm Adele," she found herself answering, though she

hadn't intended to give out any personal information to people she didn't know on this little sojourn to the far side of the station.

"A beautiful name for a beautiful lady."

The bartender groaned. "You need to brush up your lines, Dave. That one's as old as the core." The other men around them laughed and David smiled good naturedly. He seemed used to the ribbing from his comrades and paid it no mind.

"Doesn't make it any less true." His gaze held hers and for a moment it felt like only the two of them existed in the whole universe.

To read more, get your copy of **King of Swords** today! The *Jit'Suku Chronicles* books now available include:

King of Swords
King of Cups
King of Clubs
King of Stars
End of the Line
Angel in the Badlands

# *RESONANCE MATES*
## **HARA'S LEGACY**

*It's a serious game of cowboys and aliens when three psychically gifted brothers try to protect the one fragile, empathic woman who holds all their hearts against a menacing alien threat.*

Montana rancher Caleb O'Hara's precognitive abilities saved his family from an alien attack that annihilated almost everyone on Earth. Now the aliens have come to study the remnants of humanity. Caleb knows the only way to ensure the safety of his young wife, Janie, and his beloved brothers, Justin and Mick, is to keep the family together on their isolated ranch.

All three O'Hara brothers love Jane. They grew up next door to the young, empathic beauty and she stole all their hearts at one time or another, though she married Caleb. Caleb foresees the shocking truth of what they have to do in order to survive, and Caleb's visions never lie.

They'll have to come to terms with a new world, and an evolving relationship, all while finding a way to protect two newborn babies who are innocent pawns in the aliens' deadly game. Somehow, this one talented family holds the key for humanity's survival on this new, conquered world called Earth.

"Justin is mad as a hornet about something," Caleb said as he smacked his work gloves to rid them of the perpetual dust. He laid his hat aside and took off his jacket as he stomped inside the big kitchen, greeting his wife with a smacking kiss.

Jane put her coat on and picked up a wire bucket. "I have to get the eggs anyway, maybe I'll try to see what's up with him."

Caleb stayed her with a hand on her arm. "He's in a foul temper, Janie. Don't let him upset you."

She patted his hand and reached for the doorknob. "I won't. But Caleb, he needs a friend."

Caleb muttered as he watched her traipse down the path toward the chicken coop and the barn nearby where Justin kept his Harley.

"What he needs is a woman," Caleb muttered out loud, knowing Jane couldn't hear him, trying hard not to let guilt flood his mind. Jane would be back like a shot then, and he would have to explain why he felt guilty about being the only brother with a wife.

He'd tried desperately to hide the fact that the larger part of the guilt came from the fact that he felt he'd stolen Jane out from under Mick's nose, or that he suspected Justin would have courted her too, had he been home at the time her daddy died. Caleb felt like a heel. He was supposed to protect his little brothers, not cheat them out of the best woman in the world.

At the time though, he'd figured they would find other great women and settle down. Now though, with the shortage of women of any kind, the prospects were grim, and Caleb felt worse each day and each night he spent in Jane's loving arms.

Caleb watched her through the kitchen window, but staggered a moment later, as he was hit with a wave of precognitive vision that clouded his senses as it hadn't done in years. At least not this strongly. Not since the dire vision of the alien invasion had he been gripped so tightly by his gift and he slumped into one of the hard wooden chairs, letting the vision take him where it would. Surrendering to his vision, he almost feared what he might see, but resolved to use his gift to protect his family - the most important thing in his life.

* * *

Jane collected the eggs, setting the pail down on a shelf where it would be safe while she went to find Justin. He was really touchy lately, and mostly refused her offers of friendship and a friendly ear, but if she got close enough to him, she could read his emotions and at least give Caleb some clue as to what might be wrong. Caleb was the problem solver of the family, but he needed something to go on before he could put his quick mind to work to find a solution. Jane's empathic powers had provided those much needed clues in the past and she didn't mind helping him in this small way if it meant she could help the other men as well. She loved them all and she wanted them to be happy.

Jane knew Justin usually hid himself in the big stall he'd arranged to house his Harley and the various tools he needed to keep it in prime condition. It was about the size of one of the large birthing stalls in the barn, but unlike the rest of the building, it was spotless, with nary a piece of hay in sight. The concrete was a little oil stained, but there were good lights in there so Justin could easily see into the engine of his beloved machine. There was also a huge stack of spare parts and fluids that he had managed to stock up on before the cataclysm that would ensure the machine functioned well for the next twenty years at least. Caleb's precognition had allowed them to stock up on all sorts of things that were unavailable or hard to get now.

Jane approached slowly, seeing the light on through the

partially opened door. Justin had made this small room his very own retreat. There was a space heater, a comfy chair, and a small cooler with the bottled beer she'd learned how to brew for her men. They'd loved that little surprise, she knew, and a smile dawned on her face as she thought of their incredulous reaction when she'd served up the first batch a few months ago.

The door was ajar just a few inches and she approached cautiously. Justin's temper was so unpredictable, though she knew he would never hurt her. Still, she didn't want to alienate him. She hated when he turned away from her. Only Caleb could console her when Justin's anger made him shut her out and of course, then Caleb would have words with Justin for hurting her tender empathic feelings and only make the situation worse. If at all possible, she wanted to come out of this encounter with nothing more than the information she knew Caleb would be waiting for, and no overwhelming emotions that would cause further strife between the brothers.

She edged forward, into the small patch of light that was spilling into the dark barn.

"Justin?" she asked tentatively, not wanting to startle him. His reactions were lighting quick and she'd learned not to sneak up on him unless she wanted to risk bodily injury.

"Go away Jane."

The words held anger and she heard a frantic sort of rustling as she pushed the door wider to peer inside. It was obvious what she had interrupted and her face flamed red. Justin's magnificent tattooed chest was bare, his fly was open, and his hand was barely covering his thick erection.

She was caught, like a deer in headlights, her mouth forming a perfect O of surprise that only made things worse. "I'm sorry," she said quickly, feeling waves of his anger, desire and turmoil that literally took her knees out from under her.

He saw her begin to crumple and moved to catch her. "Dammit Jane," he growled as he caught her behind her knees, bringing her into the room and placing her on the overstuffed chair he'd been sitting in. He left her there while he tried to tuck in his stiff cock and force the zipper up, but it hurt like hell and when she gasped and he looked up to see her wide eyes watching him, he nearly came right then and there.

"Justin," she said softly as he turned away. "I'm sorry. I just... got overwhelmed for a moment with your anger." Her lovely, sympathetic eyes made him squirm. "I'm so sorry."

He knew he had to get himself under control or risk hurting her more. Her damned empathic senses were too closely attuned to the O'Hara boys. She'd always been able to read him like a book and he knew his anger and turmoil could hurt her.

To read more, get your copy of **Hara's Legacy** today, wherever books are sold! The *Resonance Mates* series consists of:

Hara's Legacy
Davin's Quest
Jaci's Experiment
Grady's Awakening
Harry's Sacrifice

## TALES OF THE WERE ~ THE OTHERS
### ROCKY

*On the run from her husband's killers, there is only one man who can help her now... her Rock.*

Maggie is on the run from those who killed her husband nine months ago. She knows the only one who can help her is Rocco, a grizzly shifter she knew in her youth. She arrives on his doorstep in labor with twins. Magical, shapeshifting, bear cub twins destined to lead the next generation of werecreatures in North America.

Rocky is devastated by the news of his Clan brother's death, but he cannot deny the attraction that has never waned for the small human woman who stole his heart a long time ago. Rocky absented himself from her life when she chose to marry his childhood friend, but the years haven't changed the way he feels for her.

And now there are two young lives to protect. Rocky will do everything in his power to end the threat to the small family and claim them for himself. He knows he is the perfect Alpha to teach the cubs as they grow into their power... if their mother will let him love her as he has always longed to do.

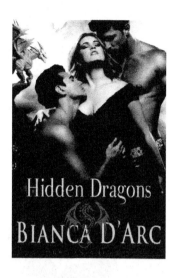

## *DRAGON KNIGHTS*
## **HIDDEN DRAGONS**

*Love flourishes when two knights unexpectedly find the woman of their dreams...*

Sir Robert finds a beautiful maiden sobbing by a small waterfall. She proves to be a very special woman who can communicate with dragons. She lives alone in the forest, on the edge of a village Robert and his fighting partner, Bear, have been sent to investigate. When she invites them to shelter from the rain in her barn, they accept, using her place as a vantage point for their surveillance of the town below.

Both knights are drawn to the fair maiden. Could she be the one to share their lives? Their dragon partners certainly think so.

When they discover a treasonous plot in the village, they must act quickly. Will they be in time to stop the enemy from gaining a strategic foothold in their land? And will they be able to protect the woman who has become precious to them, even while the battle rages?

When the dust settles, can they convince her to stay in the Lair with them...forever?

WWW.BIANCADARC.COM

CPSIA information can be obtained
at www.ICGtesting.com
Printed in the USA
LVOW04s1514251115

464205LV00022B/836/P